Bitter Pill

Books by Richard L. Mabry, MD

Novels of Medical Suspense
Code Blue
Medical Error
Diagnosis Death
Lethal Remedy
Stress Test
Heart Failure
Critical Condition
Fatal Trauma
Miracle Drug
Medical Judgment
Cardiac Event
Guarded Prognosis
Doctor's Decision
(coming this winter)

Novellas
Rx Murder
Silent Night, Deadly Night
Doctor's Dilemma
Surgeon's Choice
Emergency Case
Bitter Pill

Non-Fiction
The Tender Scar: Life After the Death of A Spouse

Bitter Pill

RICHARD L. MABRY, MD

To all the pastors, all the church workers,
all the lay individuals whom I've been privileged
to know. Your efforts are not wasted, even though
we may not see the results.

AUTHOR'S NOTES

Before I had ever published a novel, I entered an online contest held by agent Rachelle Gardner. For the best first line submitted, she'd provide her editing services. I won with the line, "Things were going along just fine until the miracle fouled them up." When I sent Rachelle the first chapter of the book that eventually became *Code Blue*, her response was, "Send me something that needs editing." That led to her accepting me as a client, and I never stopped writing. Twelve novels and five novellas (this is the sixth) later, I'm still amazed.

I've kept the outline of this novella on my computer for quite a while. A person whose judgment I trust said repeatedly, "This isn't a typical Richard Mabry novel." I rewrote it several times, and after showing the first chapter to several people they felt that it should see the light of day. I hope you agree.

My wife, Kay, has served as my beta-reader for all of these books, and I owe her more than I can say. Her knowledge and suggested comments have made this a novella of which I'm proud. I hope that you not only enjoy it, but that it speaks to you.

In addition to Kay, my thanks—as always—to the others responsible for this one: Virginia Smith, Barbara Scott, Dineen Miller, and Rachelle Gardner. And, of course, *Soli Deo Gloria*—to God alone be the glory.

1

Bob Bannister, still wearing his suit pants and an unbuttoned, sweat-soaked dress shirt, sat in the small room he was using as an office. His jet-black hair was tousled. Through the closed door, he could hear the sounds of the last stragglers filing out of the old Albertson's that was now the Faith Tabernacle of Goldman, Texas. Bannister had a glass of amber liquid at his elbow, but he ignored it to focus his attention on the sheet of figures in front of him.

A noise from the back of the room made him look up.

"Got a second, Brother Bob?" Randy Futterman was standing in the partially open doorway. Where the man had spent most of his adult life, there was neither privacy nor manners, so talking about knocking or the meaning of a closed door was an exercise in futility.

"Sure. Come in and close the door." Good old Randy, sometimes a bit slow on the uptake, but devoted as an old hound dog. Of course, some of that loyalty came from Randy's status as a wanted man. One phone call from Bannister could probably put him back in prison. However, so long as he did what he was told, the man performed adequately as an assistant.

Randy removed his baseball cap and held it in front of him like a shield. He took three hesitant steps into the room, halting several feet from where Bannister sat.

"Uh, about tonight's service," Randy said.

Bannister picked up his glass and took a sip. "Yeah, it went well. Give that woman something extra before you put her on the bus."

"Uh, uh … that's just it. We can't do that."

Bannister put down the glass—actually, he slammed it onto the table he used as a desk, some of its contents spilling onto the sheets before him. His voice rose. "What do you mean? After every service, it's the same routine—old one out, new one in. You know how it works."

"I know," Randy said. "But there's a problem."

"Why? We've always put that person on a bus out of town as quickly as possible. We don't want to risk people recognizing them and asking questions."

Randy twisted his cap with both hands. "Yeah, I know. But … you see … the thing is, somehow this lady slipped by the ushers to get into that front row seat."

"I don't understand."

"She wasn't the person we planted." Randy's Adam's apple did a dance as he swallowed twice. "I think you really healed her."

"Mrs. Ferguson, I'm so sorry." Dr. Abby Davis felt her stomach knot. She reached across the desk and covered the hand of the woman seated across from her. This never got any easier. And as young people moved away from Goldman, leaving behind a progressively older population, she was seeing more patients like this.

"I wish the news were better." Abby looked down at the sheets of paper centered on her blotter but didn't read them—there was no need. The words had burned themselves into her brain when she'd first seen them. "I just got a report this morning from the oncologist. The cancer's still growing. Your tumor didn't respond to radiation, and none of the chemotherapy drugs have helped. Nothing has worked." Abby tried to swallow, but the lump in her arid throat refused to budge. "At this point, what the oncologist suggests is palliative care—perhaps in a hospice."

Only the old woman's eyes showed her hurt. Her countenance continued to display the composure Abby had come to admire, the serenity she displayed in the face of each bit of terrible news.

Mrs. Ferguson nodded. Her voice was steady. "You're saying he thinks you should try to keep me comfortable while you wait for me to die."

The knot in Abby's midsection seemed to grow. "I don't... That's not..." She took a deep breath, pursed her lips, then exhaled slowly. "I guess so."

After what seemed like an hour, Mrs. Ferguson patted Abby's hand. "Dr. Davis, I appreciate everything you've done. I guess there's no need for me to keep seeing that cancer doctor. But can I come back to you if I need to? The pain's not too bad right now, but when it gets that way, I'm going to need some help." She looked into Abby's eyes. "And I trust you."

Abby cleared her throat and swallowed twice before she spoke. "Sure. I can see you as often as necessary. I'll stay in touch with the oncologist, and if there's something more he recommends, you and I can discuss it."

Had she made a mistake, sending this patient to the consultant she felt was the best choice? When the news of what happened to Mrs. Ferguson reached Dr. Willis—and she was certain it would—she wondered if he'd say something to his colleagues about it. Something like, "I understand that another one of Dr. Davis's referrals didn't respond to treatment. She should have sent her to me."

For a brief moment, Abby wondered if Willis was right. The oncologist she'd recommended was sympathetic and understanding, a far cry from the impersonal, assembly line practice Willis ran, but in the end nothing had worked.

Mrs. Ferguson put both hands on the arms of her chair and began to push herself up. When she paused in the process, Abby rose and started around the desk to help. The woman waved her hand and eased back down into her chair. Abby could see beads of sweat dotting the older woman's forehead.

"I'll be okay if I just rest a bit."

Abby paused where she was. She knew there were other patients waiting, but she wasn't going to hurry this woman. "Take your time." She came around her desk and took the side chair next to her patient.

Sometimes Abby thought these were the hardest moments for a family practitioner, at least for someone who cared—as she did. When it came to taking care of patients for whom there was no hope, she'd never learned to be comfortable with the situation.

Finally, Mrs. Ferguson rose slowly from the chair. "I think knowing you're there for me makes it easier."

Abby wished she could say the same for herself.

The waitress poured coffee for Scott Anderson, and although he and Ed Farmer had met in this coffee shop every Monday morning since he'd moved to Goldman, Texas, three months ago, she asked, "Cream?"

He replied, just as he'd done for about a dozen Mondays. "No thanks. Just black."

When Scott assured her that Pastor Farmer would arrive soon, the waitress nodded. "I'll keep an eye out for him. He likes his coffee hot."

Scott—he had dropped the "doctor" in front of his name when he left his surgery practice—wondered how much longer he could continue this. It was what he'd let himself in for when he decided he was taking this route. Friends told him that his decision to step away from medicine when Erica died was taken in haste, but he couldn't be talked out of it.

"Give it a few weeks," they'd said. "You've got a nice practice. Don't throw it all away." But Scott remained steadfast. Entering seminary had seemed a good way to take a year or more away from medicine, but the deeper he'd gotten into his classes, the more he had no desire to return to his surgical practice. Whether following God's call or merely reacting to a huge shock, Scott continued with his studies.

Being older than the majority of his classmates in seminary didn't seem to hurt. He'd managed to keep up with the others and even climbed to the top quarter of the class by graduation. But there were still times when Scott had been on the verge of quitting. Each time though, whether due to his inertia or by God's hand, he'd continued on the course he'd set out to pursue.

There was no question in Scott's mind that his call to become associate pastor of the First Congregational Church of Goldman, Texas, was due in no small part to recommendations from several faculty members at the seminary.

Before Erica's death, he had started growing the pseudo-beard, the "designer stubble" that was popular at the time. She thought it made him look distinguished, and he'd continued it, even after her death.

At his interview, Pastor Ed Farmer had commented on Scott's "near-beard." "It makes you look older, more mature. Keep it." So, he had.

The position seemed almost too perfect. The city of Goldman was close to the Dallas-Fort Worth Metroplex, yet still small enough to appeal to Scott, who grew up on a farm in the Texas hill country. The duties weren't onerous, and although the salary wasn't much in comparison with what he used to earn as a surgeon, the chance to listen to Ed Farmer, to talk with him outside the pulpit, as well as listen to him preach, was a great opportunity.

So far, the work hadn't been challenging—visit the hospitals and shut-ins, meet with various committees when Ed either had a conflict or manufactured one, teach an occasional Bible study class. But he knew that eventually he'd have to do more than the busywork that kept him occupied.

"Sorry, I'm running a bit slow this morning." Ed slid into the black-vinyl booth opposite Scott and almost before he'd fully settled himself, the waitress was there, brandishing her coffeepot.

"I knew you liked your coffee hot," she said, filling up his heavy ceramic mug. Then she turned away with a self-satisfied air.

Scott watched Ed Farmer do what he always did with a fresh cup of coffee; he pursed his lips and blew over the surface of the mug. Usually he followed that with, "They serve this coffee too hot." But this time was a bit different. Without looking up, Farmer said, "Scott, I want you to preach this coming Sunday."

The coffee shop was noisy, so Scott leaned across the table to be sure there was no misunderstanding. "You want me to preach next Sunday?"

"Yep." Ed took a sip of coffee and frowned. "They serve this coffee too hot. It needs to cool a bit more." He shoved the cup to the side.

"Me? Preach?"

Ed looked up and smiled at his associate. "Yes. You know—stand in the pulpit, read the Scripture, pray. They did teach you about that stuff in seminary, didn't they?"

"Yes, but—"

"No buts. I figure it's about time. You've been serving as our associate pastor for three months now. You're doing a good job, but some of the congregation are asking when they'll hear you from the pulpit. Besides . . . well, let's just say I have my reasons for getting you into action as soon as possible. So, I want you to preach this Sunday."

"If you think I'm ready—"

Farmer held up his hand, palm out, like a traffic cop. "You're more than ready."

Scott's brain went into high gear, seeking a way out. "Since I'm fresh out of seminary . . . This is my first real pastoral position, and . . . I . . . I really need some more time."

"Nope. This is Monday. You've got six days to prepare, just like I have every week. That should be enough time for you." Once more, Ed blew across the surface of his coffee cup before taking a cautious sip.

"I don't—"

Ed's laugh sounded loud in the coffee shop. "God created the world in six days. Surely, you can get a sermon ready in that time."

"I … I'll do my best."

The senior pastor tried his coffee again and found it drinkable this time. He swallowed at least a third of it before setting his partially empty mug on the table and wiping his lips. "Let me know if you need any help—books in my library, sermon outlines from my files—but I think you'll be fine."

Scott managed to keep up his end of the conversation as it turned to the local sports teams, but in the back of his mind he was once more asking the question, *What am I doing here?*

Now it was time to stand and deliver—in this case, to deliver a sermon from the pulpit. And that's where the trouble might lie. Because in the sermon Scott figured he was going to be called on to reveal the depth of his own beliefs. And right now, he wasn't totally sure what his beliefs were founded upon, or how deep that foundation went.

The prowler moved from shadow to shadow in the postmidnight darkness. About an hour ago, the clock had rolled over from Monday night to Tuesday morning. The neighborhood was quiet as people slumbered, some anticipating what the remainder of the week held, others dreading it. School was back in session after the summer hiatus, the children were all asleep, and now the parents had joined them. Every house on the block was silent. Nothing stirred. Perfect for what the prowler had in mind.

A few faint lights glowing through the windows marked houses whose inhabitants liked the security of a night-light—sometimes to soothe a child, or to facilitate trips to the bathroom or kitchen. But the windows of the house that was occupied by his target remained dark. Good.

The prowler didn't know whether this particular garage was full of junk, or the car's owner was too lazy to do more than stop at the curb. In either case, the gray Toyota sedan that was his target tonight was parked outside. So much the better.

By the faint light of a distant streetlamp the prowler could see evidence of a fine dusting on some of the cars at the curb, dirt combined with pollen from the ragweed that was still blooming here in Texas in early fall. He could imagine that, if the owners washed off the ash he was about to create, the benefit would be clean cars. Well, all except one, which would be incinerated.

The prowler's first thought had been to blow up the car by lighting a gasoline-soaked rag stuffed down the filler neck of the gas tank. But a little Internet research convinced him that maneuver was more successful in movies and books rather than in real life. Okay, he could adapt. He'd douse the front seats of the car with an accelerant, toss in a match, and run. That should deliver the desired message.

What message? The same one he'd tried to communicate by a few telephone calls and anonymous notes. The prowler had talked with people in town whom he thought believed as he did, that the man sleeping inside that house was a threat to the people who heard him. They listened politely, but no one would take action. Well, he would! And since what was going on was obviously the work of the devil, sending the message via fire seemed quite appropriate.

The prowler carried a pinch bar in the rumpled gym bag in his hand, ready to pry open the driver's side door or break a car window for access if needed. But that proved unnecessary. The car was unlocked. Either the driver felt safe and secure, or simply didn't care. In either case, this stroke of luck made his job easier.

His supplies nestled inside the bag, which now rested on the pavement. The prowler carefully extracted them, one by one, forming a neat row on the sidewalk—a couple of cans of charcoal lighter fluid, a box of kitchen matches, an old towel.

He looked around once more, checking the neighborhood. All quiet. Well, that was about to change.

The prowler was poised to proceed when a sudden noise made him look up. Three police cars screeched to a halt at the end of the block, their helter-skelter positions at the curb, indicating a bust or robbery in progress. The headlights of the cars stayed on, partially illuminating the people who emerged. A couple wore civilian clothes; the others were clad in police uniforms with jackets displaying the words Goldman PD in large reflective letters on the back. The revolving strobes on top of two cars and flashing from behind the grill of a third painted the area in splashes of red and blue.

This wasn't the best of neighborhoods in Goldman, and it took only a couple of seconds for the prowler to fit the pieces together. For whatever reason, the police had picked tonight to raid the house at the end of the block. Which was all well and good in most circumstances, but not tonight. The prowler didn't need their presence while he was preparing the conflagration he had in mind—and certainly not while he made his escape afterward.

As the police fanned out around the house at the end of the street, the prowler took three deep breaths to still his rapid *heartbeat.* Don't let panic make you do something stupid. *If he remained calm, he could sneak away undetected. In the space of a few seconds, he carefully returned the items to his bag and then eased away until he was completely hidden in the shadows.*

The prowler turned and peered from his hiding place in the darkness. No one was looking his way. He edged further away, using the cars parked at the curb for cover, pausing at each one to make certain he was unobserved. Finally, he started to walk down the sidewalk, holding the bag against his side, both to conceal it and still its faint rattle. When he left the shadows, the prowler walked purposefully toward where he'd left his car.

He reached his vehicle, which was headed away from the police activity at the far end of the street. He climbed in, then experienced a moment of panic when his car failed to start on the first try. He turned the key again and breathed a silent sigh when the engine turned over and caught. Using only his parking lights, he pulled away from the curb. Soon he was driving toward freedom. He felt frustration that he wouldn't be delivering the warning tonight. But there'd be another time. And he trusted that the conflagration he had planned would get the message across to Bob Bannister.

2

Bob Bannister struggled to escape his nightmare. It didn't seem to matter that he knew in some deep recess of his mind that it was only a dream. The anguish and fear he felt were real.

In the dream, he was wrestling with the devil, just as Jacob did with an angel in the Bible story. Bannister vaguely recalled the story from Sunday school. But this time the wrestling match wasn't for a blessing, like the one that happened nearly four thousand years ago. The stakes were even higher. Bannister was wrestling for his eternal soul. And he was losing.

"If I win, I get your soul," the devil said in a deep voice that sounded like that of James Earl Jones.

Bannister panted, fighting to breathe through the constricting embrace of the fiend.

"And if I win?"

Satan laughed. "No need to think about that. You have no chance."

The more Bannister squirmed, the more he struggled, the tighter the devil's grip held him. Finally, just as he thought he was breaking free, he came awake with a start.

He looked around, taking a moment to orient himself. He was entangled in the bedclothes, which were soaked with sweat.

He had just looked at the bedside clock, seeing that it was almost two in the morning, when he heard a commotion outside. Was that what woke him? After listening for a moment, Bannister thought about looking out his bedroom window, but then decided it had nothing to do with him. He straightened his sheets as best he could, crawled back under them, and managed to fall asleep, only to drop into the same dream.

This time, Bannister was able to break free, but not before his heart was again pounding like a trip-hammer. He decided there was no reason to try to sleep any longer. He swung his feet over the side of the bed and slid them into slippers. Pulling the bedspread around his shoulders like a cape, he made his way to the kitchen of the house he occupied rent free, courtesy of one of the faithful attendees at Faith Tabernacle.

After making coffee, Bannister wandered into the living room, collapsed in a chair, and considered his dream. There was no need for in-depth analysis by some Freudian psychiatrist. The meaning was clear to him. He'd had similar dreams—really, nightmares—in the past, but tonight's had shaken him to the core. Could the dreams have been triggered by the woman who responded to his tug on her wrist, first standing, then walking, and finally almost dancing out of the Tabernacle, leaving her wheelchair behind? He knew he was a fraud, but he'd managed to ignore the consequences … until now.

Although Bannister's initial thought had been that the woman was a better actor than the usual shills, when he learned it hadn't been a setup, troubling thoughts tumbled through his mind in earnest. Who was she? Was the woman an investigative reporter of some type, participating in the healing to gather information? Was an exposé coming? He wondered if he'd have any kind of advance warning before it was made public—perhaps a call from the newspaper or TV station. And what would follow that revelation? He knew the answer to that, as well as the preemptive action he was prepared to take to prevent the consequences he would face.

Bannister had very few possessions, and those could be thrown into a suitcase quickly. He could be in his car and on his way out of town in less than an hour. His retinue would follow as soon as he called Randy and told him where they'd next meet up. There was always another town several counties down the road, another site to set up shop. But was that what he should do now? What was he waiting for?

There was another possibility, of course, one that was much more troubling. Had he really healed her? And if he had, what did that mean? Was it a sign? Of what?

He was still sitting in the living room chair when he heard the knock at the door. He ignored it until the knock became a pounding, accompanied by a loud voice.

"Police. Open up."

For almost twenty years, since the death of Abby's parents in a fire that claimed both their lives but spared hers, Aunt Kay had been the closest thing she had to a mother. So, when Abby was deciding where to set up her practice after graduation from medical school, she couldn't ignore the yearning in her heart. Thus far, she hadn't regretted moving home to Goldman.

Ordinarily, she and her aunt would have had dinner together on Sunday evening. But since Aunt Kay had to cancel their long-standing appointment this week, they had rescheduled their meal for this evening. They were seated at Aunt Kay's table, but Abby was too preoccupied to enjoy the food and the conversation. Struggling with her thoughts, Abby finally decided to share the problem. "Aunt Kay, I don't think I can continue doing this."

"Continue what?" Kay said.

Abby took a tiny bite of mashed potatoes. "Today a woman with terminal cancer said she wanted to continue seeing me, even after all the consultants have said there's nothing further to do for her."

"Did she think there was something you could offer?"

"Nothing medical. I guess she wanted my assurance I wouldn't abandon her." Abby lifted her glass of iced tea, then put it back down without drinking.

"Well, that's good," Kay said. "What's the matter, then? Do you think that if she doesn't get better, you've failed her?"

Abby shook her head no. "I guess not. And I'll pray for her, although I know that sometimes God's answer is to heal the person in heaven, not on earth." She frowned. "But..."

"But what, dear?"

"But what if, despite her hopeless situation, this woman *does* get better? What does that tell me?"

"Does it matter?"

Abby thought about that. "I guess not."

"You don't worry about whether she gets well or not. Just support her in prayer. Leave the rest to God."

On Tuesday evening, Scott Anderson sat in his tiny apartment and tried not to fall asleep over his books. Despite his best efforts, periodically he started to nod and the words on the pages in front of him blurred, their meaning escaping him. He hadn't pulled an all-nighter in quite a while—not in med school, not in the seminary—and he didn't plan to do it now.

Nevertheless, he felt as though his eyelids were made of lead. It seemed that his mind wanted to escape the task before him and drift elsewhere. He leaned back in his chair, stretched, and looked at his surroundings.

When he first came to the church, Ed Farmer had taken him to a tiny, windowless room there and explained there simply wasn't anywhere else to put the office for the new associate pastor. "But you won't be in it much. You can study at home—I'm sure you have most of your books from seminary there—and you can use my office anytime you need to."

"Thanks," Scott said. "I'll be fine with this plus working from home."

As it turned out, the "home" Scott occupied here in Goldman was a tiny apartment—just a bedroom, bath, cramped kitchen, and small living room. At first his reference books had been left in several boxes in a corner of that living room. Ed's request that Scott needed to preach on Sunday led to the unpacking of those books, an event that he'd hoped to put off indefinitely. Now most of his textbooks and notes had been emptied from the boxes and were strewn and stacked on the kitchen table where he sat.

Was his current situation really what he wanted? For what seemed like the millionth time, he wondered if he'd made the right decision. At the time, it seemed to make some degree of sense. His friends had tried to talk him out of it, of course. Who but an absolute idiot would walk away from a flourishing surgical practice and apply for admission to seminary? But that's what he'd done. When you get right down to it, it was probably in response to a single mistake—a mistake that he felt cost his wife her life.

Scott felt tears stinging his eyes. Because no one was around, he let them flow. He cried for the family he'd never have. He cried for the guilt he still felt about his wife's death, and the way he felt he contributed to it. He cried for the faith that once was his rock, but now was more and more a façade he put on like his "preacher suit" before heading for church.

In a moment, the weeping subsided. He fished a handkerchief from his hip pocket and wiped his face, then blew his nose. Scott felt that his life was like that handkerchief—used up, unclean, dirty. What would it take to make it like new again?

He shook his head. Better get on with his studies. During his years at seminary, he'd heard lots of sermons in chapel. He had dozens of books written by famous preachers. Surely, he could take the salient points of one of these messages, flesh them out, pad them with buzz words that would show the congregation he was well-grounded in hermeneutics and exegesis and all those terms. But in the end, it would be meaningless. One of his profs, he couldn't even recall who, had said that good sermons came, not from the head, but from the heart. And his heart was empty.

Scott had yet to come up with a sermon—title, topic, Scripture, anything. This was Tuesday night. Sunday morning was fast approaching, and he had nothing. He pulled a Bible—one of several translations he owned—from the pile of books on his desk.

He riffled through the pages, stopping when he saw a passage he'd highlighted with a yellow marker. Scott read it, rapidly at first, then again slower. He smiled, because he'd found his sermon topic. The Scripture serving as the basis for what he said would be Isaiah 30:21: "Whether you turn to the right or to the left, your ears will hear a voice behind you, saying, 'This is the way; walk in it.' "

He pulled a pad toward him, turned to a blank page, picked up the pen he'd been chewing on, and wrote at the top of the sheet his sermon title: "Help me, God, I'm lost."

Early on Wednesday morning, Bannister sat at the kitchen table, staring into space, his third or fourth cup of coffee cooling before him, when he heard the tap at the backdoor. He roused himself long enough to check the clock over the stove: 9:00 a.m. Until now, he would have assumed the person at the door was Randy. Until recently, he'd thought not many people knew where he was staying, or even cared. But he'd been proven wrong.

Should he have looked out the window? Why bother. What was the use? "It's unlocked."

The kitchen door eased open and Randy came in. As always, his brown eyes constantly darted right and left, but today his ocular gyrations were combined with a hangdog look that said, "Don't blame me. I'm just the messenger."

"What's wrong?" Bannister asked.

"Uh..." Although Randy usually stopped about three or four feet in front of Bannister, today he stayed beside the kitchen door, apparently poised to turn and run at any minute.

Bannister slowly rose and moved to stand directly in front of Randy, invading his confederate's personal space, his six-foot-two frame towering over the smaller man. He tried to look less menacing but could see that he wasn't succeeding. When he put his hand on Randy's shoulder, he felt the underlying muscles quiver like those of a dog when it's afraid of being kicked.

"I asked you what's wrong," He kept his voice neutral, but emphasized the question by a slight squeeze of Randy's shoulder.

"You…you didn't hear nothing outside last night?"

"Tell me."

"Your car."

In the same way that a faithful follower of his ministry provided this house rent-free, another had loaned Bannister a 2007 Toyota Corolla. The car wasn't much to look at, and it burned through a quart of oil about every 700 miles, but it provided adequate transportation within the city.

"What about my car?" Bannister's voice remained calm.

"Didn't you see it? Couldn't you hear the commotion? It…it burned up."

Without a word, Bannister turned away and walked slowly out of the kitchen, with Randy several cautious steps behind. At the front window, he parted the slats of the venetian blinds and looked out to see his car, or at least, what was left of it, standing at the curb on four melted tires. He'd seen this earlier, right after the police knocked on his door, but at that time the car was illuminated by headlights. Now, in the daylight, the full extent of the damage was evident.

The car's usual color—tan with a few spots of primer— was an uneven charcoal, mixed with a few residual areas where the paint had blistered but was still recognizable. Everything inside the car appeared destroyed—dashboard, seats, everything. He wasn't certain about the engine but had no desire to lift the hood and look. The damage was total.

Bannister wondered if this would have happened if he'd put the car in the garage last night. But, as usual, he'd been too tired to bother. Then again, would it have mattered? He shook his head.

"Didn't you know?" Randy asked.

Bannister didn't answer at first. Then he spoke in a surprisingly quiet voice. "I knew. At first, I ignored the noise outside. I guess I figured it had nothing to do with me." He turned away from the window and dropped onto the sofa. "The pounding on my door got me up. I talked with the police—although I might not have made much sense because of… because of what I'd had to drink and the sleeping pill I took. After they left, I've just been thinking."

"So, would you like me to line up another car for you?" Randy asked.

Bannister shook his head. "Not yet. I don't know how much longer we're going to be here." He looked up at Randy. "Cancel the next service. Put a sign on the door. Give the band and ushers Saturday night off."

Confusion marched across Randy's face. "What … what do I tell them? When will services start again?"

The reply was accompanied by a slight, sad shake of Bannister's head. "I don't know. I don't know what I'm going to do."

After Randy left, Bannister moved to the desk in the corner of the front room, opened the middle drawer, and pulled out the notes. First the anonymous phone calls, then the notes. Maybe he should have heeded them, should have headed out of town after the first or second warning. But something, the same kind of stubbornness and curiosity that makes a child touch a hot stove or makes wet paint irresistible to an adult despite the warning sign, had kept him here.

He probably should have shown the notes to the police, but he didn't want them delving too deeply into Randy's background ... or his own for that matter. Better to attribute the burning of the car to a random act.

"No, officer. I have no idea who might have done this."

All three notes were similar—a single sheet of lined paper torn from a child's tablet bearing words that had been scrawled with a soft lead pencil. Each note was printed, maybe written by a right-handed person using their left hand to avoid identification. Nevertheless, Bannister could easily read the words. Actually, he didn't have to read them now—he remembered them all. With only slight variation, they all said the same thing.

STOP WHAT YOU'RE DOING OR PAY THE PRICE!

The most recent one had been slid under his front door sometime during the night. He saw it when he let the police in and shoved it, unread, into the waistband of his shorts and covered it with his T-shirt before he opened the door. This one was different than the others:

IF YOU DON'T LEAVE TOWN, THE NEXT TIME IT WON'T BE YOUR CAR THAT BURNS!

Abby glanced at the schedule of patients that Gloria had placed on her desk. This Wednesday morning, like every morning, would be full, not just with the people whose names were listed here, but the unexpected ones—emergency cases that would need her attention. She did her best not to keep patients waiting, but Abby generally considered herself fortunate if she finished a morning's list by half past twelve.

On other days, this might necessitate snatching a sandwich at her desk so as to be ready to get back to work by one. But today was Wednesday, her afternoon off, so she'd probably have time for a less hurried lunch. Beyond that, though, there was no telling what lay in store for her.

A light tap at her office door made her look up. "Yes?"

Ruby eased the door open and entered the office. She held a thin stack of pink message slips. "No important messages when I checked in with the answering service. All but one of these is for the okay of a prescription refill. I'll give those to Gloria."

"And the one that isn't?"

The receptionist handed Abby a slip that contained a name and phone number but no message. Abby studied it, then looked up at Ruby. "No reason given for the call?"

"Nope. I can check, but I figured you'd eventually want to talk with him."

Abby nodded. "You're right. I'll call him now. After that, I'll be ready to start seeing patients."

Ruby closed the door behind her. Abby picked up her phone and punched in a number. In a moment, a man's voice answered.

"Pastor, this is Abby Davis. You called?"

"Thanks for calling me back," Ed Farmer said. "Would there be sometime today when I could come by your office to chat?"

Abby scanned the schedule on her desk. "Certainly. I could work you in—"

"Abby, let me interrupt. This isn't something that will require your examining or treating me. I just need about half an hour of your time to discuss something. And if we could do it today..."

She frowned. "I suppose so." Abby doodled a question mark in the margin of her schedule. What could Pastor Farmer want? Well, she'd see soon enough. "Why don't you come by at noon?"

It was about a quarter past twelve when Ruby stuck her head into Abby's office. "That was your last patient." She frowned. "And Reverend Farmer's in the waiting room. I don't see his name on the books? Are we working him in?"

Abby swept a lock of chestnut hair out of her eyes. She'd need a haircut soon, but she wasn't sure when she'd find the time. Maybe tomorrow she'd put her hair up in a ponytail, if it was long enough. That should buy her a little time. "No, he just needs to talk with me. You and Gloria go ahead and close up. I'll bring him back to my office myself."

As Abby escorted her pastor down the hall, she heard Ruby checking out with the answering service. Theoretically, Abby wasn't on call for the rest of the day. As a practical matter, she knew there'd be at least a couple of calls that began, "Dr. Davis, I know you're not on call, but..." And she'd take them. After all, what else did she have to occupy her time?

She directed the pastor to a chair, thought about taking her usual seat behind the desk, then changed her mind. She took the chair beside him, turning it so they were facing each other. "What can I do for you?"

"Abby, we've known each other for about five years—ever since you came here to set up your practice, I guess. I've learned that I can rely on your discretion, and I'm going to ask you to keep what I tell you today in confidence."

Abby frowned. Several possibilities ran through her mind. Had the pastor gotten himself in some kind of trouble? Was he about to confess a particularly grievous sin to her? No reason to keep guessing. She'd know soon enough. "Of course. What is it?"

"When you did my annual physical about a year ago, everything seemed fine."

She nodded.

"But recently, I've had some problems."

Abby started to swing into full doctor mode, asking about her pastor's symptoms, but he forestalled that with an upraised hand.

"I told you, this isn't a professional visit, and you'll see why in a moment. I noticed a tendency to sometimes drop things, but I attributed that to clumsiness. I occasionally had trouble remembering words, but I figured this was normal for someone who was over sixty. I attributed a bit of weakness in my left hand to the same thing—advancing age. But eventually, Florence said I had to stop ignoring the symptoms. She made an appointment in Dallas at Southwestern Medical Center."

"I trained there—good people," Abby said.

"I agree. I saw a doctor in the General Internal Medicine Department—really nice guy, seemed to know his stuff." He grimaced. "He put me through a rigorous physical exam, then ordered a CT scan of my head. He said I might need some more tests, possibly have to see another doctor in a different department at the medical center."

Warning bells went off in Abby's head. "What did he think?"

"I could tell he was worried. Since then, I've had an MRI, an ultrasound, some other tests. Yesterday, I saw the man he referred me to. A neurosurgeon. He thinks I have an aneurysm."

"Of the brain?"

"Yes. A weak spot in a vessel, sort of like the bulging of a balloon. And it's in a delicate spot in the brain."

She was already thinking about what this might mean. "So, what's next?"

"If it bursts, it's probably not a survivable event. If he operates, the surgeon might be able to clip it, although there's a chance... Well, there are possible residuals." He hesitated. "Or I might die."

"Have you decided what you're going to do?"

Farmer nodded. "I'm having the surgery, but I talked the neurosurgeon into giving me some time to get things in order. I'm scheduled for a craniotomy next week." He shrugged his shoulders. "The church will be okay while I'm gone. You've met my new associate, haven't you?"

"I've shaken hands with him a few times. But let's talk about you. When is the surgery exactly?"

The pastor pulled out his phone, punched a few buttons, and gave her a date.

"That's next Monday," Abby said. "Are you satisfied with that opinion? Do you want to see someone else? I can set that up."

"No, I think the folks at Southwestern have handled this perfectly," Farmer said. "And I'm prepared to follow the advice I give my congregation: hope for the best, prepare for the worst, and turn the problem over to God."

"Then what can I do?"

"Remember what I said? I'm hoping for the best, I'm prepared to face whatever comes, and in the meantime…"

Abby nodded. "Turn it over to God."

"Right." Her pastor shifted in his chair. "I want someone I can talk with about this. Someone to pray with."

"Why me?"

The pastor looked her in the eye. "Rose Ferguson told me you promised to take care of her, even though all the consultants have pretty much given up hope. Actually, I guess you're acting as her prayer partner. That's giving her great comfort." He fiddled with the knot of his tie. "I'm going to leave this matter with God, but I'd like to have a prayer partner as I go through it."

"What about your wife?"

The pastor frowned. "You're not married, are you?"

Where was this going? "What does that have to do with anything?"

"I love my wife. I tell Florence everything. I've told her about this, but I've tried to paint it in the best possible light." He leaned forward and lowered his voice. "You're a physician. Like a pastor—like me—you've been around a lot of people who are dying. I'd like to spare her the anguish I sometimes feel. But I need to share it with someone."

"So, you want me to—?"

"Just be there for me. Let me call you when I'm down. Pray for me." He paused. "Pray with me."

Abby gave an inward sigh. "Of course, I'll meet with you, talk with you, pray for you and with you." Her hands shook slightly as she held them out, palm up, to her pastor. "But you're not expecting my prayers to heal you, are you?"

"The Bible tells us that the fervent prayers of a righteous man can do a lot. I suspect that goes for a righteous woman as well." The Reverend Farmer leaned forward and took Abby's outstretched hands. "I think your help—and your prayers—are what I need to get through a really tough time. And should God choose to heal me, I wouldn't object. Would you?"

Abby thought of a number of ways to turn down the request, but after a few seconds, she simply said, "Of course not."

Farmer shook his head. "We're told in Scripture that walking in the footsteps of our Lord isn't a path of ease. Quite the opposite. But I don't think any of us are prepared for the bitter pill we're sometimes asked to swallow. This is one of those."

3

D r. Ben Crabtree gestured for Abby to take a seat across from his desk. "I appreciate your coming by my office on your afternoon off."

Abby bit back the retort that was on the tip of her tongue. Ben was probably sincere in thanking her for making time for him today. He probably never considered the implication carried by a phone call to her from the chief of the hospital's family practice section.

"I feel as though I've been summoned to the principal's office," she said.

"Relax. You know my position is mainly honorary, Abby. But sometimes I'm called on to deal with a problem, and it's often distasteful." Crabtree leaned back in his office chair and frowned, probably at the message he was about to deliver.

Abby waited patiently. Finally, she decided to help him. "Look, obviously whatever you called me here to tell me is something you'd rather not pass on. Just spit it out. I'm a big girl."

"I've heard a complaint about you, and I want to talk with you about it," Crabtree said. He immediately held up his hand. "Not a formal complaint. But something you've been doing that isn't going over too well with your colleagues."

Abby felt her hackles rising. After trying so hard to be a responsible family doctor. After putting in all the effort. After... Never mind. "Who doesn't like it? What did they say?"

"I'm not at liberty to divulge the identity of the person who made the complaint."

She sat up a bit straighter in her chair. "I'm not sure how I should respond to an anonymous accusation."

Crabtree appeared to like the situation less and less. "Abby, this isn't a courtroom. I'm not really dealing with you as the chief of the family practice section at the hospital. We're just two colleagues... two friends talking. I've heard some things that might cause you trouble and wanted to pass them on. Okay?"

Abby took a deep breath and tried to calm herself. "Okay. So, say what you need to say."

"You've developed a habit of referring patients to doctors other than those in our own medical community. And I've heard some complaints about that practice."

Abby tensed. She was ready to get up and walk out of Ben's office, but she realized this was more painful for him than for her. He was sincerely talking with her as a friend. "I see. And do I get three guesses as to the identity of the complainant? I only need one. Dr. Carlton Willis."

Ben looked like he'd swallowed something sour. "I can't say."

"You don't have to. Yes, I'm referring patients to a doctor who doesn't use this hospital. Carlton Willis couldn't make a living as a surgeon here, so he let out the word that he was specializing in patients with malignancies. If he could operate on them, he did. If his surgical exploration showed an inoperable disease, he sent them to a local radiologist who administered radiation and then sent them back to Carlton. Sometimes he could decide that without surgery, but Carlton usually came down on the side of, 'Let's operate and see what's there.' "

"Let me—"

Abby kept on talking. "After that, if they needed further treatment, they got chemotherapy according to one of about three standard regimens he got out of some medical journals. But at no time...nowhere...did they get a friendly word, a listening ear, or a compassionate doctor who'd talk with them about their problems." She paused and drew a deep breath. "Is that the doctor to whom you want me to refer my patients?"

Crabtree's face reddened progressively during Abby's speech. "I'm not saying you're right or wrong about the identity of the doctor, but the medical community you and I represent, the doctors who are on the staff of this hospital, well, they're a pretty closely knit group. It's tough enough for a specialist to make it here, with Dallas just a short drive away. When local doctors fail to consider that type of patient flight, I think you can see where it might ruffle a few feathers."

"Do you refer your patients who need an oncologist to Willis?"

"What I do isn't the point here." Crabtree suddenly stood, walked to the door, and made certain it was closed. Then he turned back to Abby. "This isn't to be repeated, Abby. No, Willis isn't my preference for patients with cancers. But I also give those patients a choice. I have the names and addresses of three oncologists, in alphabetical order, printed on sheets of paper. His is one of them. He's local, although he has nothing to support his calling himself an oncologist. The other two are fellowship-trained in that subspecialty and practice less than a half-hour away. But I don't set myself up as judge and juror about what Willis does." He returned to his chair and slumped down behind the desk. "I'm simply asking you to be a bit more circumspect in handling this situation."

Abby nodded. "I see. I guess I can try to be a little fairer. But most of my patients ask me for my personal recommendation, and I will continue to give it."

"And one thing more," Crabtree said. "There are some rumors circulating that you're trying to heal some of your patients through prayer."

Abby realized this might not be the time or place to get into a long discussion with Crabtree. "Not at all. I pray for myself—for wisdom and ability—and I certainly don't hesitate to pray for my patients. I even pray with them, if they ask for it. But I don't try to heal them that way."

Crabtree appeared bound to take it further. "So, you're not saying that healing comes from God?"

"On the contrary, I believe all healing comes from God. He just chooses to use medical means most of the time. I believe the French surgeon, Ambroise Paré, said it very well: 'I dressed the wound. God healed the patient.'"

Crabtree smiled. "In medical school, one of my professors said that God heals the patient, while the doctor sends the bill."

Abby opened her mouth to reply but shut it without saying anything. No reason to take this further right now. Meanwhile, she'd been put on notice about referrals and

Dr. Willis. She would have to be more cautious in her actions. But her basic philosophy wouldn't change.

"Thank you for seeing me this evening." Bob Bannister looked around at the room where he sat. "And it's especially kind of you to do it at your home, not your office at the church."

Pastor Ed Farmer wasn't at all what Bannister expected. Rather than a dress shirt and tie, the man wore a sport shirt and jeans. When he propped one foot on the hassock in front of him, worn cowboy boots came into view. And Bannister couldn't recall meeting a minister with so many laugh lines in his face, accented by a booming voice and a ready smile. This was a man who loved life. How long had it been since Bannister had that feeling?

"No problem. And I hope you don't mind that I've changed into more informal clothing. I don't believe a preacher should wear a tie every day, although I'm sure some people in my congregation would be happy if I wore one with my pajamas."

Bannister smiled. "As I said, you're very kind even to see me."

Farmer leaned back in his chair and laced both hands over his midriff. "I'll be honest with you. Your call came as a complete surprise to me." The pastor looked up at the ceiling. "You'll have to admit that this is sort of like the chairman of one company coming to see the CEO of a rival."

"I guess we are competitors of a sort," Bannister said. "Or, at least, we used to be."

The pastor brought himself slowly upright, put two feet on the floor, and leaned forward toward his visitor. "Maybe you'd better explain that to me."

Bannister looked behind him to make sure that the door to Farmer's study was closed. Then he spoke in a voice that was just louder than a whisper. "I don't have to tell you what kind of services I've been holding at Faith Tabernacle for the past three months or so."

"Yes, and I'm surprised you aren't getting ready for Saturday's service," Farmer said. "That's your big night, isn't it?"

Bannister masked his surprise that Farmer knew the schedule of his services. He guessed it was time to get to the reason he'd consulted the man. "I've canceled the services for this weekend. And I don't know if I'll be doing any more in the future."

"Do you mean the preaching, which, when you get past the trappings that go with it, seems to be fairly biblical, although basic? Or are you referring to that bit of show-manship at the end of each service, where you choose some-one planted in the audience to be healed?"

How did he know all that? "We ... That is, I ... Well, thank you for what you said about the sermons. My past has given me a pretty good grounding in the Scriptures, at least for a layman, and I try not to go too far afield," Bannister said. "But it's the healing I want to talk to you about."

Bannister knew he appeared in control and self-pos-sessed when he stood at the podium during his services, but here, sitting within a few feet of someone who was truly a man of God, he began to sweat. He felt like an ill-prepared student before the teacher's desk. Well, he'd started this pro-cess. He might as well finish it.

He watched Farmer's face as the story unfolded—the carefully orchestrated healing services, beginning with the planting of a well-coached individual among the others who came forward at the end of the service, followed by the healing itself, and finally the surreptitious spiriting out of town of the person who was "healed" so another could take their place.

"But something went wrong last week."

"What's that?" Farmer asked.

"I thought the person who was healed gave a great performance. But as it turns out, maybe it wasn't a performance at all. The woman we planted … we couldn't find her afterward, although we looked in the usual spots."

Farmer nodded but didn't say anything. Was the man ever going to talk? Bannister wanted him to do something—bless him, reassure him, tell him the reason behind all that happened. But he merely sat silent.

Bannister swallowed twice before resuming his narrative. "I thought maybe this was some sort of investigation, perhaps by a magazine, a newspaper, a TV station. I kept waiting for the phone to ring, someone asking for my comments before they ran the story. But nothing has happened so far. Eventually, I wondered if … Well, maybe the person healed was …" He couldn't say it.

"You think God had a hand in what happened?"

"I've been having nightmares. In the most common one—the one that comes back frequently—I'm wrestling with the devil for my soul. One night, I thought I felt the fires of hell. Actually, that was the night someone burned my car in front of my house. And that same night, this note was slipped under my door." He pulled the latest note from his pocket and handed it to Farmer.

The pastor looked at it, then handed it back to Bannister. "Have you told the police about the notes?"

"No."

"I guess what I'm wondering is why you've come to me. How can I help?"

Bannister put out his hands, palm up. "I don't know. But you're the person I immediately thought of to bring my problem to."

"Because it involves the spiritual? You know, I don't really have any special connections that I can employ for you. All I can do is give you my best advice."

"I'm not sure what I'm seeking," Bannister said. "But I'm sure I can't go on this way."

"That's probably right. You need to change the way you do things." Farmer leaned back in his chair once more, his pale blue eyes fixed on Bannister. "You really want my advice?"

"Please."

"Keep on preaching the best Bible-based message you can. Stop the healing services for now. And open yourself."

"Open myself?" Bannister demanded, his voice rising. "How do I do that."

"Let me say it another way. Surrender yourself. Make yourself available. Ask God to show you what He has in mind for you."

Bannister was shaking his head before Farmer stopped. "He can't use me."

"Why? Because you've done some bad things? If God didn't use flawed people, who would He have to work with?"

Scott left the church building at lunchtime on Wednesday, telling the church secretary he'd be working on his sermon at home.

"I'm looking forward to hearing it," she said.

I hope you still feel that way after I preach it.

On the drive home, Scott thought back to the time when Erica had come in from what he'd thought was a routine visit with the gynecologist. True, she'd had a few complaints, but Scott didn't think much of them.

He still could feel the emotions that crowded in when she told him what the gynecologist had told her—disbelief that her complaints were indicative of a serious condition, thoughts of who he could have her consult for a second and even a third opinion, and in the back of his mind, the realization that what he heard constituted a virtual death sentence for his wife.

They'd confirmed the diagnosis—Scott knew in his heart it was accurate—and began a fight that lasted about a year, employing every tool available through modern medicine to fight the disease. Through it all, Erica had tried to reassure Scott that her condition wasn't his fault. He couldn't have seen it coming.

Just as they had before her health declined—perhaps even more—they talked about their dreams for the future. "We'll beat this," he'd said.

Scott mentioned a short mission trip. Perhaps that would give Erica something to look forward to. As she continued downhill, he made bargains with God, bargains that eventually involved trading his life for hers, but despite efforts that could only be described as heroic, she'd lost her fight.

Afterward, Scott sank into the depths of depression. He'd had enough of medicine. He tried, but he discovered that he couldn't face the inside of a hospital again—not as a physician, anyway. One of the bargains he'd made with

God, if He'd spare Emily's life, was to devote his own life to the ministry. Even though his wife had died, perhaps he should take this step now anyway.

After several weeks of soul-searching, Scott applied for admission to a seminary. His friends and colleagues told him he was crazy to change professions. Did he know what this would mean? To leave his practice and attend seminary? He knew nothing of what that life entailed. They pointed out, as best they could, the changes in his world that lay ahead of him. Yet Scott remained firm in his resolve. He could get through it, just as he'd navigated the study and long hours associated with medical school.

At first, Scott enjoyed the challenge and the change. As graduation drew near, he wondered what he'd do, but things just seemed to work out. He sat down with the pastor and elders of this church, gave all the right answers, and responded to their call to fill the position of associate. But now it was time to put up or shut up. It was time to preach. Was it too late to pull out? How could he tell Ed it had all been a mistake?

Standing in the pulpit meant having the depth to his faith to draw on as he fed the flock before him. But his faith was like some of the rivers in Texas during a time of drought—broad enough to look good on the surface but without any real depth.

When he arrived home, Scott headed for his kitchen table after grabbing a bottle of water from his refrigerator. Soon the yellow sheets in front of him were filled with notes that resembled the result of dipping a chicken's feet in ink and setting it loose over the paper. Several Bible translations and commentaries, a few books from his seminary days, and a couple of volumes of collected sermons by preaching giants of the past ringed the table where he was putting together his thoughts, such as they were.

Although he'd tried writing his sermon draft using his laptop computer, Scott had soon abandoned that. He found that he did better transferring his thoughts to paper via longhand. He intended to put things in their proper order and produce a typescript eventually. He just hoped he'd be able to do all that before Sunday.

He had another idea, one at least marginally connected to what he'd been writing, and he hurried to jot it down before it left him. Just as he tried to capture the thought, his phone rang. He ignored it, something he'd never been able to do in the four short years he'd been in medical practice. He'd check the caller ID in a few moments and return the call if it were important. It was probably a spam call anyway. That seemed to be the main thing he received on his landline.

He looked off into the middle distance before scribbling, "These are the signposts God has planted along the way for us to use when we lose our way." He'd transition to an anecdote of being lost on a hiking trail—

Scott's train of thought was interrupted again by a noise. This time it was his cell phone buzzing in his pocket. Before he even looked at the caller ID, Scott knew it was from the church. They were the ones who usually called him on that phone. He punched the button and identified himself.

Ed Farmer's voice came through as though he were in the same room. Matter of fact, sometimes Scott wondered why the pastor used a phone. Why didn't he just open the window and shout? From the pulpit, even when he spoke softly, it was possible to hear every syllable he uttered all the way to the last row of the sanctuary. Scott made a mental note to ask him about that sometime.

"Making any headway on that sermon for Sunday?" Ed asked.

"I've got a title, and I know the points I want to make. I was working on the lead-in when you called. Thanks for asking."

"Are you free for lunch tomorrow?"

"Ed, I'll probably still be working on my sermon. I don't think I should take time for lunch."

"Come on, man. We've all got to eat."

Scott felt like pulling out his hair. How could the man be so calm? "Ed, it's Wednesday afternoon already, and I don't have Sunday's sermon finalized. How do you get it done in time?"

The smile in the pastor's voice came through just as though he were standing next to Scott. "Son, by the time Monday ends, I know what I'll say the next weekend, and I have a pretty good idea of how I'm going to say it. But it took me years to get there. Given a little seasoning, you'll get there, too."

"But I want to say the right things."

"Don't fret about the words you'll say on Sunday. The message will come to you. And if it comes out right, they won't be your words. They'll be God's. Just let yourself be the messenger and see how things flow."

Scott wasn't sure the advice helped any, but he appreciated the encouragement. "Thanks, Ed."

"Meanwhile, let me pick you up at a quarter to twelve tomorrow. We need to talk."

Despite the encouraging message Ed had delivered, those words made him frown. "We need to talk? If this were a dating relationship and I heard those words, I'd think I was in trouble," Scott said. "But I'm not ... am I?"

"I guess that depends," Ed said, all the humor gone from his voice.

A wisecrack jumped into his mind, but Scott bit it back. Instead, he said, "I'll see you tomorrow."

After Scott ended the call, he didn't reach for a reference book or a Bible or one of the volumes of sermon compilations. Rather, he looked up at the corner of the room and tried to imagine what the pastor wanted to talk about. But he soon gave up.

The answer's not written on the ceiling, Scott. Just wait and see.

4

The problem with having a half day off in the middle of the week is that there's always paperwork on your desk demanding attention when you get back. At least, that was what Abby Davis thought on Thursday. And she certainly didn't feel rested as she worked her way through the material piled up for her before seeing the patients who were scheduled for this morning.

She wondered how her pastor was doing today. She was still worried about him—doubly so—because not only did he have a potentially fatal problem, but all she could do was watch from the sidelines as other doctors took over.

Added to that, she had tossed and turned all night, angry about the meeting with Dr. Crabtree and her frustration with Dr. Willis. Even though she'd felt exhausted by the time she fell into bed, she couldn't stop the freight train of thoughts rolling through her head. So, all in all, today wasn't a great one for her.

She was just finishing with a patient when she heard her name called from the doorway.

"Dr. Davis?"

Her receptionist Ruby didn't normally interrupt unless it was important. Abby continued to hold the twisted ankle of the woman on the examining table. "Yes?"

"I have a walk-in who seems pretty sick."

Abby looked up. Ruby had been around long enough to know when someone needed the doctor's attention right away. "I'll be right there."

She turned back to her patient. "Neither the X-ray nor my exam show any fracture. It's just a sprain."

"I'm glad to hear that, doctor," the middle-aged and obviously obese woman on the exam table said.

"Sprains are as painful as a break though—sometimes more. You need to stay off your feet until you can put weight on it. If supporting it with the elastic bandage doesn't work, we can go to a walking boot, or even crutches."

The woman eased off the exam table onto her good foot, then gingerly tried to put weight on the damaged ankle. "That's better. But I think I'd feel more secure using the crutches you mentioned."

"No problem," Abby said. "Gloria, give Mrs. Gunderson a pair of crutches and show her how to use them properly." She turned back to the patient. "If you have any questions, ask Gloria. And let me see you here in a couple of weeks for follow-up. Of course, call earlier if there's a problem." *And I'll need to advise a weight-reduction diet before this happens again.*

In the hall, Ruby pointed to the treatment room across the hall. "He came in complaining of chest pain and shortness of breath."

"Thanks," Abby said.

The man sitting on the edge of the examining table looked vaguely familiar, but Abby couldn't place him. He was pale and sweating, and his respirations were more gasps than inhalations. Maybe he was having a heart attack. Or maybe it was something else.

"Just lie back," she said, reaching for the oxygen mask hanging on the tank beside the table and hooking him up. "I'm Dr. Davis. Tell me when this started." As they talked, she shoved his sleeve up and applied a blood pressure cuff.

"I've been … I woke up this morning feeling … my chest hurts. I can't get a deep breath," he gasped out, his voice muffled slightly by the plastic mask over his mouth and nose. "Am I … having a heart attack?" He grimaced. "Am I … going to die?"

"Not right now," Abby said. She took the stethoscope from around her neck. His blood pressure wasn't low, as she'd expect with a heart attack. Actually, it was higher than normal. His pulse was a bit rapid and very strong. His respirations were rapid, almost gasping. "I want to check a cardiogram," she said. "Just try to relax, Mr.… I'm sorry. I don't think I have your name."

"Bannister," the man said. "Bob … Bannister."

Ed picked Scott up at noon on Thursday. Scott didn't ask about their destination, instead joining in a casual conversation. But when it became obvious where they were headed, he looked at Ed and shook his head. "Somehow, when you told me you were taking me out to eat, I pictured us going to a nice restaurant. Maybe even the country club. But what I see ahead of me is a row of fast-food places. Is that where we're going?"

"Do you have something against What-A-Burger?"

"Not really," Scott admitted. "I like What-A-Burger."

As the pastor steered his Ford F-150 into a slot outside the small white building, Scott turned to him and said, "Ed, let me ask you about the vehicle you drive. Every time I see you in this pickup truck, I wonder why you're not driving something more … more in keeping with your position."

Ed put the transmission into PARK and turned off the ignition. "My position isn't any different than anyone else's. People are wrong when they put a preacher on a pedestal. I like driving a pickup, so that's what I do. Besides, this is Texas, where a pickup is more common than a Lexus in most places."

"I didn't mean to offend you," Scott said.

"No offense. I'm sure there are a lot of people in the congregation who would like to ask that same question. They just don't have the temerity, I guess, to voice it."

"Sounds like you're pretty comfortable in your own skin. I wish I were as comfortable about the sermon I'm going to preach on Sunday."

The pastor obviously wasn't in a hurry to trade the quiet of the pickup for the noisy interior of the restaurant. "Scott, I know how worried you are about that. And all the assurances in the world aren't going to make it any easier for you. But if you're sure it's the right thing for you to remain in the ministry, nothing is going to stop you."

"Thanks. But why did you put that disclaimer in there? Don't you think my surrendering to preach is in accordance with God's will?"

Ed turned a bit to his right and put his arm along the backrest, not quite on Scott's shoulder. "I know you gave up your surgical practice to enter seminary. When others tried to pin you down on your reason, you talked about answering a call. But a couple of your professors at the seminary told me they believe you applied because you blamed yourself for failing to recognize the symptoms of your wife's ovarian cancer. When she died, they think you went into the ministry as penance." He paused. "Is that the case?"

Scott remained silent. Right up to the time Erica died, she told him repeatedly not to blame himself—but he did. And perhaps his decision to enter the ministry really was an attempt to make things right. But surely his action wasn't wrong.

"Maybe you're right," Scott said. "But if that was the case, why did the seminary accept me as a student? And why did you offer me this job?"

"The seminary admissions committee can decide whether you have the qualifications. The faculty can decide if you're prepared. But none of them can look into your heart and see what's there. Some of the faculty at the seminary thought they saw something special in you, which is why they recommended you for this job. And I saw it too. I think there are great things ahead for you. But, whether it's in the pastorate or back in medicine, well, we don't know yet." Ed paused. "Do you?"

Scott didn't know what to say. He'd wrestled with that question for quite a while, but he still didn't know the answer.

"Anyway, I didn't mean to hit you with all that. Actually, I simply wanted to give you a heads-up. You're likely to be called on to preach more often in the future. And your duties at the church may increase pretty soon."

Before Scott could ask what Ed meant, the pastor opened the door of the pickup and said, "All that serious talk has made me hungry. How about a cheeseburger and fries? Maybe a malt to wash it down? We'll talk as we eat." Ed moved to Scott's side and put his arm around the younger man's shoulder. "I just hope what I tell you doesn't make you lose your appetite."

Abby felt certain that the signs and symptoms her patient exhibited constituted an episode of hyperventilation as the result of a panic attack—not a heart attack. After she looked at his EKG and confirmed her impression, she'd left him with assurances she'd be back soon to check on him. "I want to watch you for a bit. Is there a problem with your staying here a little longer?"

"I guess not," Bannister said. "And you'll be right next door?"

"I promise you," Abby said. "But push the button on the wall there if you need me."

After she'd taken care of her last patient for the morning, she told Ruby, "I'll be in the exam room with Mr. Bannister. You and Gloria go ahead and get some lunch. Just bring me back a sandwich."

"Will you want one of us—"

"Don't worry. I'll leave the door open," Abby said, smiling, although she didn't think there was any problem being alone with this man.

When Abby entered the exam room again, Bannister was sitting on the edge of the table, showing no evidence of the distress he'd displayed earlier. Abby checked his blood pressure and pulse once more. Then she nodded to herself and removed the sphygmomanometer cuff from Bannister's arm to let it hang from the rubber tubing on the wall where it was anchored. She listened to the man's heart again before shoving her stethoscope into the pocket of her white coat.

"Your vital signs are stable. Your cardiogram shows no evidence of a heart attack. I think you're okay."

"I didn't have a heart attack?"

"No, it was probably a panic attack that caused you to hyperventilate." She dropped onto the padded stool that stood at the foot of the exam table where the man sat. "And usually there's something that triggers such an episode. Want to tell me what's bothering you?"

She could almost see and hear the wheels turning in Bannister's head as he tried to decide what to share with her. Abby didn't yet know what it was, but there was definitely something there. "Let me assure you that whatever you tell me won't go beyond this office."

"I know," he said. "Unless it has to do with a crime I'm planning—sort of like with a lawyer or a preacher. I know all about that."

The fact that he said "preacher" rather than "priest" told her he was probably Protestant. And his knowledge that the "seal of the confessional" and "lawyer-client privilege" had that one condition attached to them made her look at him with new eyes.

"Exactly," she said.

"I know you're a female doctor and I'm a male, so I understand why you left the door open, but could you close it?"

Abby got up and did as he'd asked. "Now what's so secret?"

"I guess you know who I am," he said.

"All I know is your name—Bob Bannister. Should I know you?"

"I'm the preacher at Faith Tabernacle. We hold services twice a week."

She raised her eyebrows but said nothing.

"And the most noteworthy thing about those services are the healings I do at the end."

Then it came back to her. She'd read about it in the local newspaper when the church—she didn't know whether to call it a church or not—started holding healing services. But she'd read about this man. And she'd heard people talk about him. So far as she could tell, opinion in Goldman was divided between those who wanted to sanctify Bannister and those who wanted to ride him out of town on a rail.

"Anyway," Bannister said, "The healings were faked, of course. But a few days ago, I may have actually healed someone. At first, I was afraid this was part of some sort of investigation, but no one has contacted me. Then I wondered if I really healed them. If so, was it a miracle? After that, I've had repeated dreams of wrestling with the devil for my soul."

Abby held up her hand. "I can see why you'd have anxiety attacks and an episode of hyperventilation. I suppose I could give you some medicine to help with that. But you need to talk with somebody who does counseling about the underlying problem. Maybe a minister. Certainly not me."

"I did that already," Bannister said. "I talked with Dr. Farmer at the First Congregational Church."

"And…"

"He gave me some advice, and I'm still turning it over." He pursed his lips. "I'll take that prescription you talked about. Do you want to see me again for follow-up of this spell I had?"

Abby thought about the situation. She'd found no cardiac problems. And the tranquilizer she planned to give Bannister was fairly mild. But it wouldn't hurt to see him again, especially if he needed someone to talk with. And that appeared to be the main function she could serve right now.

She took a deep breath. "Certainly. Let's see you in two weeks to see if the medication has helped. But meanwhile, call me anytime."

On Friday night, Scott sat in the back row of the pastor's study and watched the elders file in and take their seats on the folding chairs that had been set up. He hadn't really had much faith that a large number of men would show up, but he was wrong. Apparently, the elders took their obligation to the church seriously. They had left their commitments to family and others to attend this special meeting called for tonight.

In the short period Scott had been there, Ed Farmer had been like a second father to him. When the young—well, relatively young—staff member stumbled, the pastor was always there with an encouraging word and good advice. But what happened after Ed's surgery? Scott hesitated to even think about it, but what if Ed weren't able to continue to lead the congregation?

When Ed Farmer stood up behind his desk and began to speak, a quiet settled on the room. Every eye focused on the pastor. Ed opened his Bible and read from Psalm 139, stopping after the sixteenth verse. Then he looked up and his gaze swept the people gathered there.

"We are all part of God's master plan. And we all have an expiration date."

Some in the assemblage saw Ed's smile and joined him in chuckling silently. "And mine may be coming up." One by one, the smiles of the men disappeared, replaced by somber expressions as the pastor's words sank in.

Ed's gaze went from person to person. "I have an aneurysm—a weak spot in the vessels at the base of my brain. I'm scheduled to have surgery by a specialist at the medical center in Dallas. What comes after that? We don't really know."

Hands immediately shot up with questions, and Ed answered each one as best he could. Finally, when no one seemed to have anything more to say, the pastor spoke again. "I've asked Scott to bring the message this Sunday, and I hope you'll be here to support him. Now I'll ask you to spend the next few moments in prayer—for me, for the medical professionals who'll be caring for me, and for Scott."

Some of the people in Goldman looked forward to Friday evening because that meant they could shed their inhibitions, relax, and enjoy the weekend. Abby Davis wasn't quite like that though. It wasn't that she didn't relax, but she did so in a different place and in a different way. Since she'd moved back to the city after getting her medical degree, she'd spent a good bit of her free time with Aunt Kay. And that's where she was tonight.

"This meal is delicious," she said, looking down at her plate where the remains of a slice of roast beef and gravy lay surrounded by mashed potatoes, buttered carrots, green beans, and two slices of tomato.

"How would you know?" Aunt Kay said. "You've hardly touched the food on your plate."

"You dished out more than I need ... or want," Abby said. "But what I tasted was very good."

"Something's bothering you. Want to talk about it?"

"I will after we've finished eating."

Kay pushed her almost-empty plate aside. "Well, I've had enough, and it looks like you're not going to eat any more." She folded her napkin and rose from the dining room table. "Leave the dishes. I'll clean up in here later. Let's sit down in the living room. You take off your shoes, relax, and tell me all about it."

When Abby had done as her aunt suggested, she said, "I'm sorry I didn't eat much of the dinner you fixed. I really haven't been very hungry lately."

"Something wrong?"

"Not really. Maybe I'm just worn out from all that's been happening."

"I know how you worry about your patients," Aunt Kay said. "But what happened this week?"

"First there was Mrs. Ferguson. I've already told you about her. She hasn't responded to the treatment of her cancer, but she wants to keep seeing me, even though there's nothing medical I can do."

Aunt Kay nodded but remained silent.

"Then there was—well, I can't tell you his name, but he's seeing a consultant at the medical school because of a possible brain aneurysm. He wants me to be his prayer partner. And finally, another man, and I guess I shouldn't tell you his name either, came in on Wednesday hyperventilating. He thought he was having a heart attack. He's ... he's involved in religion, and God is dealing with him right now."

"No wonder you're feeling under pressure."

"Aunt Kay, why do patients keep seeking me out for things other than what I learned in medical school?"

"Because you're one of the few people who'll minister to both their body and their soul. And both are important."

5

On Friday evening, Bob Bannister sat alone in the small house where he lived for the time being. A Bible was open in front of him. His conversation with Pastor Ed Farmer, followed by his session with Dr. Abby Davis, convinced him he needed to make some changes. Unfortunately, he wasn't yet certain what they were.

He looked down at the large, leather-bound volume in his lap. On the flyleaf, in his mother's copperplate handwriting, was this inscription: "To Robbie. Wherever you go, whatever you do, this will be your roadmap."

Okay, Mom. I have the Book. Where's the map leading me?

He hadn't seen his parents in over a year. He called them every few weeks, talking about trivial things. They thought he was a traveling salesman, on the road, moving around the area. Well, he guessed he was. But what he sold was hope. And now he needed to change the way he did it.

Just as Bannister thumbed through the Bible, a knock at his door interrupted him. He opened it to see Randy standing on the porch.

"What do you want?" Bannister asked, only partially successful at masking his irritation at the intrusion. He immediately regretted his tone. He had to treat people better. That was one of the changes he needed to make.

Randy removed his baseball cap, revealing his receding hairline. "Can I come in, Brother Bob?"

Bannister pasted a smile on his face. "Sure."

As Randy entered, Bannister said, "And for now, maybe you should just call me Mr. Bannister, not Brother Bob."

The man looked like he wanted to ask "why," but instead he pointed outside. "I'm glad to see someone gave you another car. I guess that means you're staying here a while."

Bannister gestured to a chair. "Actually, nobody gave the car to me. I bought that old Honda Civic with my own money. And yes, I'm staying for a while. But there might be some changes in our services."

After they were both seated, Randy said, "I guess you know what you're doing, canceling the Saturday night service." Doubt colored Randy's words. "Have you changed your mind? Shall I tell the band and ushers that the service is on? And do you want me to line up someone to be healed?"

Bannister took a deep breath. If he followed Farmer's advice, there was probably no turning back—at least, not in Goldman. "Yes, I've changed my mind. The service is on. The band might want to tone it down a bit, though. We'll take the offering at the end, the same as we always do." He felt like a man poised on the tip of the high-diving board. *Here goes.* "But there won't be a healing."

Randy's face fell. "But that's our big draw. Why are you canceling it?"

"There are some things going on that I can't explain. Just do it my way. Okay?"

After Randy left, Bannister slumped back into the chair and opened the Bible. Then he closed his eyes and said out loud, "Okay. I've taken that step. Now what?"

When Abby Davis's phone rang on Saturday morning, she was still in bed. The clock on her bedside table said five minutes after seven.

Ordinarily, she was awake and out of bed at 6:00 a.m., but last night her sleep had been troubled, interspersed with dreams about patients with problems unresponsive to treatment. The last time she recalled looking at the clock it was about five, so she'd probably been truly asleep for a couple of hours.

Abby had long since recognized that a family practitioner could expect to get calls at odd hours and even on weekends. She rolled over, fumbled for the phone, and answered the call.

"Dr. Davis, I hope I didn't wake you, but I wanted to talk with you before I left town."

The voice sounded familiar, but not distinctive. "Who is this?"

"Oh, I should have identified myself. This is Muriel Ferguson."

Abby sat up in bed. "What's the problem, Mrs. Ferguson? Are you having pain that the medication isn't relieving?"

"No, actually, since my last visit with you, I've had less pain. The reason I called is that my daughter has finally convinced me to come and live with her and her husband in Houston. They want me to see a specialist at M.D. Anderson Cancer Center. Even if the doctor there agrees that nothing more can be done, I'm going to stay in Houston with my family until ... until the end."

"I'm sure your daughter wants you near her. When you get your appointment set up with the doctor at Anderson, let my office know so we can send our records to them. You know, they have several studies going on there, and you may qualify for one of them."

"My daughter and her husband will be here later today to help me move." She hesitated. "I know it sounds silly, but I think our time together helped me. Will you continue to pray for me, even when I'm gone from Goldman?"

"Of course, Mrs. Ferguson."

After she ended the conversation, Abby thought about the woman and all the patients like her—people who had reached the end of what medicine could do for them. All that was left for them was to make their peace with God and await the end. If Abby could make that easier, wasn't it as important—maybe even more important—than what she could do with her prescription pad?

What about the ones treated by Dr. Willis? True, he probably helped some of them—maybe more than a few—with surgery where it was indicated or by prescribing chemotherapy and radiation if that would help. But did he care about them? Abby had no firsthand knowledge, but the reports that filtered back to her indicated he didn't. No matter the opposition she faced, she planned to continue to minister to patients like Mrs. Ferguson—to their body *and* to their soul.

Bob Bannister felt like he'd swallowed a whole family of butterflies, and they were trying all at once to escape from his stomach. Pre-service jitters were common with him, but these were jitters on steroids because tonight would be different. He wondered how the congregation, or audience, or whatever you wanted to call the people gathered there in the Faith Tabernacle, would react.

Instead of his usual white suit, Bannister wore one of charcoal-gray with a faint pinstripe. His shirt was white, paired with a conservative red-and-black figured tie. In the auditorium, the band played, but instead of their usual upbeat music, these were arrangements of hymns that set a worshipful mood. He'd ordered Randy to skip the introduction. After the music stopped, he planned to walk onto the platform, open his Bible, and preach.

His text was from selected Psalms. After all, David—who wrote most of the book—was a man who'd gone astray, just like Bannister had. Yet he was used by God.

I guess it's true. God uses flawed people because that's who's available. I just hope He can use me.

When Randy tapped on the door, Bannister said, "Ready?"

"All set, Brother ... I mean, Mr. Bannister."

Randy was having trouble not calling him Brother Bob. Well, Bannister had gotten used to the name as well, but somehow it no longer sounded right. Would he still be Brother Bob after tonight? Or would he even want to be?

By force of habit, Bannister reached for the glass and bottle that normally stood on a nearby table. Then he drew back his hand and smiled. He popped a couple of mints into his mouth, took a final look into the mirror, straightened the knot in his tie, and headed for the door.

It was well after midnight, but Bob Bannister wasn't sleepy. He sat in the living room of his house, his feet on an ottoman, reflecting on what had happened tonight. The service had gone well, he thought, but when he ended it without the healing—the thing that had come to mark his services—he could sense a murmuring among the crowd. Oh, no one got up and stalked out of the assembly. The people stayed for the final hymn, remained standing for a benediction, then quietly filed out. But there was no question that this change in the service was noticed. Some seemed to approve, others showed disappointment. Well, he'd just have to see—

The sound at the door wasn't really a knock. Rather, the thin wooden panel transmitted a faint scratching. Then Bannister heard a slightly louder, inarticulate sound that was more like a wounded animal than anything human. Before approaching the door, he considered looking for a weapon, but decided there was no need for it.

He turned on the porch light but couldn't see anything through the peephole. Yet the sound continued. Finally, Bannister opened the door on the security chain. He looked quickly, could see nothing, so he closed the door. The sound, a whimper interspersed with occasional scratching, started again and Bannister decided he was going to have to look outside through a fully open door.

He changed his mind and picked up a fireplace poker. Bannister held it cocked over his right shoulder, ready to defend himself against whatever was out there. He flung open the door and saw Randy, prone on the porch, right arm outstretched toward the now open door. A trail of blood led up the sidewalk from Bannister's car to where Randy lay, bleeding from multiple slash wounds on his arms and neck.

When Randy saw Bannister standing above him, a brief smile flashed across his blood-streaked face. "I tried to stop him," he whispered, and then he passed out.

Even though it was after midnight on Saturday, usually a busy time for police and emergency rooms, Bannister's 9-1-1 call brought a response within just a few minutes, minutes that seemed like hours to him as he stood over the wounded man. Should he move Randy? Was it best to cover him to keep him warm, even though the temperature outside was in the mid-seventies? Should he do something to minister to the man's cuts, which were still oozing? Was there more damage that wasn't apparent? Finally, as he waited, Bob Bannister did something he hadn't done for a long time—he knelt at Randy's side, held one of those bloodied hands, and prayed.

The police and ambulance arrived almost simultaneously. While the two patrolmen asked questions of Bannister, the emergency medical techs went immediately to work. After what seemed like an interminable time to Bannister (but was probably only a few minutes) the lead EMT straightened and said, "I think he'll be okay. Let's get him to the hospital."

Whether it was the IV fluids, the bandages on his cuts, or the fact that he was safe from any further attack, Randy did, indeed, seem a bit stronger after receiving emergency treatment. The paramedics told Bannister that, although there had been blood loss, the knife wounds weren't life-threatening. However, Randy had also been beaten.

Although he was still not feeling well, Randy insisted on relating his story to the police before he was taken away. He said he decided to take a walk after tonight's service, and his feet had led him to Bannister's house, where he saw a prowler doing something to the reverend's car.

"I should have ... called for help ... I guess," he said. "I tried ... to stop him myself. He hit me with his fists. Then, when ... I was down ... he cut me. And ... he kicked me."

"Don't talk if it tires you," the patrolman said. "We'll look around before we leave. Then we'll talk with you again after you're—"

The lead EMT interrupted the policeman. "We need to get moving!"

As the gurney rolled toward the ambulance, Randy held up one hand to stop the EMTs. "I remember the knife ... was ... funny looking."

The stretcher was moving again, with the policeman walking alongside to ask one more question. "Would you recognize your assailant?"

"I ... I don't know." Randy looked up at Bannister. "I'm sorry. I couldn't stop him, Brother ... Mr. Bannister."

"That's okay, Randy."

When everyone had left, Bannister exchanged his normal sleeping attire of T-shirt and shorts for slacks and a sport shirt. He slid his sockless feet into running shoes before going out to his car, intending to head for the emergency room to check on Randy. As he expected, the interior of the car had been slashed numerous times—front seats, overhead liner, several cuts on the plastic of the dashboard. But it was still drivable.

As Bannister pulled away from the curb, he was pretty certain this was the work of the same person who'd sent him the anonymous notes and burned his previous car. Now they'd attacked Randy. Should he just leave town? Or stay right here? He pondered that during the drive, but as he approached the emergency room entrance, Bannister still wasn't sure of the answer.

6

On Sunday morning, Scott sat in the small room that was nominally his office at the First Congregational Church. Ed Farmer had invited him to use the pastor's larger office, but Scott declined with thanks. He appreciated the gesture, but somehow it didn't seem appropriate. Especially when he still had doubts that he was going to remain in the pastorate.

Scott had dressed carefully in his best black suit and a snow-white dress shirt. Earlier in the week, he'd looked in the mirror and had a fleeting thought about using some dye to cover the smattering of gray hair at his temples, but he quickly discarded the idea. No, this was who he was. Besides, Erica once told him it made him look distinguished—that and the designer stubble on his chin.

He ran his hand across his chin, feeling the bristles of what he'd heard called his "near-beard." How much longer would he keep that look? For that matter, how much longer would he be in his current position?

His Bible sat at his elbow on the desk. His printed outline lay folded just inside the front cover. A few discreet, colored tabs on various pages marked the Scriptures he wanted to use. He knew what he wanted to say ... if he could just communicate it to the congregation.

He looked up when he heard a tap at the office door. He consulted his watch and saw that it wasn't time for services to start. Ed Farmer opened the door and said, "Am I interrupting?"

Scott beckoned him in. "Not at all. Come in and sit down."

Ed closed the door behind him and took the chair across the desk from Scott. "Nervous?"

"Of course," Scott said. "Isn't that to be expected?"

"It's not as though this were the first sermon you ever delivered," Ed said. "I seem to recall preaching several sermons as part of my classes. Of course, seminary courses may have changed since I got my degree."

"No, I've done that. But this is different. This is delivering a sermon from the pulpit usually occupied by a man I consider a preaching giant."

"Don't think about that—not the place or the person you're replacing. Think about the congregation before you. Some of them need their batteries recharged, some have never heard the Gospel, and despite your best efforts, some may leave without being touched."

Scott puffed out his cheeks and exhaled. "That's true, and I guess that worries me some."

Ed leaned toward Scott. "Your job isn't to change any of their hearts. It's to use this hour to make the Bible come alive for them, to remind them of the Gospel, and to invite those who haven't done so to accept the gift God offers. Leave the rest to the working of God's Spirit."

"I guess you're right." Scott slowly nodded his assent. "And, of course, I don't want to forget about you. Your appointment for surgery at the medical center is tomorrow, isn't it?"

"Yes. I certainly appreciate your prayers, but this service isn't about me. And it isn't about you. It's about doing what I laid out for you. Let your words be a vehicle God can use."

Ed started to push back his chair, but Scott stopped him. "Would you pray with me before you go?"

"Of course." And the two men knelt.

After the amen, Ed rose and clapped Scott on the back. "Now, as the actors say, break a leg."

Bannister spent the evening at Randy's side in the emergency room and later in a two-patient room. The doctor who had sutured the lacerations and checked Randy more thoroughly wanted to watch him overnight, including a recheck of his blood count after it had a chance to stabilize. Bannister's adrenaline level was high, so sleep was out of the question. Instead, he headed home, where he shaved and changed into a fresh shirt before setting out for the First Congregational Church. He still wondered why he was going, but there was no doubt in his mind that he needed to attend the services.

When he slipped into a back-row seat, the sermon had just started. Bannister saw that it was delivered by the associate pastor, Scott Anderson. He had hoped to hear Ed Farmer, but there was no inconspicuous way to slip out now. Instead, he listened intently. As the message progressed, Bannister felt certain the words were aimed at him. He found the sermon title in the bulletin: "Help Me, God. I'm Lost."

When the service ended, Bannister wanted to avoid shaking hands or being welcomed as a visitor, so he stayed in his seat in the rear of the church. He kept his eyes downcast, trying to look as though he were deep in reflection, maybe even prayer. It seemed to be working, because although from the corner of his eyes he saw a number of people looking his way, some even taking a few steps toward him, they veered off when they saw he was deep in thought.

How much longer until these people were gone? Well, however long it took, Bannister could wait. He looked toward the front of the church and saw Dr. Abby Davis, apparently in deep conversation with the pastor and associate pastor, talking and laughing.

The associate pastor finally left the group and headed for a door at the side of the sanctuary. Bannister figured that was the way to his office, and he slid out of his pew and eased along the wall in time to tap the man on the shoulder as he opened the door. "Excuse me. I wonder if I might have a few moments of your time."

"Sure."

"In private, if that's possible."

Scott shook hands with the people as they left the church. Some had a word for him. Others simply nodded. At least there were no negative comments. Ed Farmer had given him good advice. Prepare to the best of your ability, then let God take over. And so far, the results had seemed positive. Whether the people who sought him out after the service were just being nice, or if his sermon had really touched them, he was glad to receive their positive comments and even happier that the experience was over.

Of course, depending on the results of Ed's craniotomy, Scott might have a lot more preaching to do. But that was down the road. Right now, he just wanted to escape into the small room that served as his office, close the door, and melt into a puddle.

Scott was about to open the doorway at the back of the worship center when he felt a tap on his shoulder. "Excuse me. I wonder if I might have a few moments of your time."

When Scott turned, he saw a man in his mid-thirties, clean-shaven, with neatly combed jet-black hair. His sport shirt and slacks were clean and unwrinkled. But the bags under his eyes bore silent testimony of a sleepless night. What was the story behind that?

There was nothing overtly threatening about the man, yet Scott felt warning bells going off in his head. He looked around and saw the auditorium was virtually empty now. But he smiled, or at least tried to. "Sure."

"In private, if that's possible."

Something about the encounter continued to raise the hackles on Scott's neck. He decided to tread carefully until he knew more about this man. "Tell you what. Everyone else seems to have gone. Let's have a seat here on the front row. If we need some time alone in my office, we can arrange that for later. Right now, I'm really worn out and anxious to go."

"I know the feeling," the man said. He followed Scott to seats at the end of the first row. Both men sat down, and the visitor stuck out his hand. "I'm Bob Bannister."

The name didn't mean anything to Scott, although it seemed the man expected it to. He took the offered hand. "Scott Anderson. What can I do for you?"

"I came here hoping to hear Ed Farmer preach," Bannister began. "But when I saw your sermon title in the bulletin, I knew I was in the right place." He held up the worship guide and pointed to the printed title of the sermon.

Scott remembered how the title had come to him, and the internal struggle that preceded it. "Help Me, God. I'm Lost," he said. "Yes. I was preaching to myself, as well as to everyone in the congregation who felt that way."

"And I'm one of them," Bannister said.

"I'm sorry to hear that," Scott said. The next words came automatically. "How can I help you?"

"I've already told my story to Ed Farmer, but after hearing you this morning, maybe you'll have a few words of advice for me as well."

"I'll try."

"It didn't seem as though you recognized my name," Bannister said. "You may have heard of me as Brother Bob Bannister, pastor at the Faith Tabernacle here in town."

Now Scott realized why the man seemed familiar. He'd seen his picture on flyers posted throughout town when the Tabernacle opened a few months ago. "I see. So that's why you said you were familiar with what I'm feeling right now. I guess that happens to you as well."

"Oh, you haven't heard the story yet. You see, I used to have a healing at the end of every service…"

The congregation had left the church building almost a quarter of an hour ago, one or two even sliding toward the exits during the closing prayer. It was Ed Farmer's custom to stay until everyone was gone, then slip back to his office for a few quiet minutes before joining his wife for lunch. But today he'd leave it to Scott to greet the attendees. He was ready to leave.

Despite himself, he found his thoughts turning to his surgical procedure tomorrow. He continued to hope that the craniotomy would reveal something that could be dealt with easily, that he'd come out of the anesthetic with no residuals. But each time he experienced difficulty remembering, a weakness in his hand, all the things that had led him to the consultation, he had to work to avoid sliding into the slough of despond that John Bunyan described in *Pilgrim's Progress*.

As he looked around the nearly empty building, he thought of what he could do to keep his lunchtime conversation with his wife from deteriorating into a "poor me" monologue. Then he made a decision. He'd invite Scott Anderson to join them. Scott had done a great job with the sermon, and Ed had been one of the first to shake his hand after the service was over. But he knew from experience that Scott would spend the next hour or more dissecting his message, wondering about things he might have done differently. Eating with the Farmers might keep him from doing so much of that. And Florence wouldn't mind.

Ed headed for Scott's office but pulled up when he saw the associate pastor sitting in the front row, deep in conversation with Bob Bannister. Ed couldn't hear what was said, but in a moment, Scott put his arm around Bannister's shoulder and both men bowed their heads. The prayer was almost a whisper, so Ed had no idea what was said. But he bowed his own head, and when he heard the men rise from their seats, he whispered, "Amen."

Bob Bannister went back to his house and found the note on the front door. He had received messages before, usually slid under his door. The wording varied, but the message was the same. But this mode of delivery, and the message that went with it, was unusual and upsetting. Very upsetting.

The note had been printed in pencil on a sheet of lined paper torn from a child's tablet just like the others. But although previous notes had been delivered in a more conventional manner, the delivery method sent a cold chill up his spine. This note had been affixed to his front door with a hunting knife driven deep into the wood! Obviously, the person sending the message meant to send a deadly warning.

Bannister looked around, but there was no one in the area. By and large, his neighbors kept to themselves, which wasn't unusual since he'd quickly figured out that some of those people were on the wrong side of the law. He couldn't complain, given that the house was being provided for him rent free, so he'd followed a live and let live policy. At any rate, he decided it would be fruitless to ask if anyone had seen the person who did this.

Should he notify the police, let them see the note and knife in place before he removed them? No, Bannister figured he should have involved the police much earlier. He hadn't, not wanting to draw law enforcement attention to himself. Now he'd probably lost his chance. He'd keep this one to himself as well.

He worked the knife free, but not before he noted that whoever drove it home was quite strong. He had to use both hands to eventually pry it free. Since he'd decided the police weren't going to be involved anyway, he didn't worry about fingerprints. Bannister unlocked the front door, shoved the knife into the drawer of an end table, and turned on the overhead light to read the note. There wasn't much to it, but it told him, he should continue to watch his back.

The message on the note was a bit longer than the others, but equally blunt and threatening.

DON'T THINK OMITTING YOUR SO-CALLED HEALING FROM ONE SERVICE WILL MAKE ME STOP. GET OUT OF TOWN, OR ELSE!

At midmorning, Abby Davis took advantage of a break in her schedule to head down the hall to her office. On the way, she grabbed a bottle of water from the workroom refrigerator. Once inside with the door closed, she dropped into the chair behind her desk and held the cold bottle to her forehead for a moment. Then she opened it and took a healthy swallow. It was a usual Monday, which meant she'd been busy all morning. If one of her patients hadn't failed to show for his appointment, she wouldn't have had this brief breather.

Although she'd been occupied all morning with the medical problems facing her, occasionally her thoughts would drift to Ed Farmer and the surgery he was scheduled to undergo today. She wondered if she should call University Hospital in Dallas and ask about him. Despite HIPPA rules that protected patient privacy, she was a physician who had trained at that facility, and Abby felt sure she could wangle some information about Ed's case one way or another. But she resisted the temptation.

Ed's wife had Abby's cell phone number and had promised to let her know when she had some information to pass on. But so far, there was none.

"Dr. Davis."

Abby looked up and saw her nurse standing in the doorway.

"Yes, Gloria?"

"I'll put your next patient in a room in a few minutes."

After several years together, Abby was pretty good at reading non-verbal cues from Gloria. "Is there something on your mind?"

"Any word on Pastor Farmer?"

Abby shook her head. "I've been expecting a call. I even started to phone the hospital but decided it's probably too early to know anything."

"Let me know when you hear," Gloria said. "In the meantime, I'll just keep praying."

Me too. Just like I've been doing since Ed told me about all this.

As Abby rose to follow Gloria, her cell phone rang. She glanced at the face of the phone and saw the call was from Florence Farmer. "Florence, this is Abby. What's the news?"

"I ... It's not good."

Florence's words were followed by sobs, and Abby could almost see the tears running down the woman's cheeks. She didn't want to hear what came next, yet like the motorist who slows down to look at the carnage of a car wreck in the opposite lane, she had to know. "What is it?"

"The surgeon ... The doctor just came out ... He told me."

Abby felt like she was pulling teeth, but she gently asked, "Told you what?"

Florence sobbed into the phone, and it took a moment for her to control them. With a sinking heart, Abby already knew what Florence wanted to say. She closed her eyes when his wife choked out, "Ed's dead."

7

Scott Anderson sat in the cramped confines of his church office on Monday afternoon, his desk piled high with books, pages marked with Post-It notes, along with scraps of paper bearing his scribbles. The yellow pad in front of him remained as blank as his mind as he searched for the right words to say when he preached at the memorial service for his friend and pastor, Ed Farmer.

When the chairman of the elders called him earlier that day with the news that Dr. Farmer had died, Scott wondered which of Ed's pastoral colleagues would preach the funeral. Later he was told that Ed's widow—the word seemed strange when applied to Florence Farmer—wanted Scott to bring the main message.

Later, Abby had reached out to him with the news of Ed's death. She'd talked with the neurosurgeon who had performed the operation and was able to give Scott the details of what happened. Ed died on the operating table, not as a result of his aneurysm, or even the craniotomy to address it, but due to an unexpected cardiac event.

Before surgery, Ed's medical status checked out. He had no symptoms of heart problems, his EKG was unremarkable, his lab work spot on, and an internist at the medical center had pronounced him healthy enough for surgery. But while the neurosurgeon was performing the procedure, Ed's heart had gone into ventricular fibrillation—the sudden change from a rhythmic, purposeful beat to a quivering of the heart muscle that robbed it of pumping action. There had been no response to medications, electroshock, even opening the chest and directly massaging the heart. Despite measures that could only be described as heroic, the pastor was ultimately pronounced dead.

What was doubly sad, of course, was that just before Ed's episode, the neurosurgeon had exposed the aneurysm and felt he could handle the problem while causing little or no residual effects in the patient. But before the doctor could complete the operation, Ed was dead from cardiac arrest.

Scott had always hated knowing as a surgeon that he could have saved a patient, but unforeseen events resulted in death. On those occasions, he had to break the news to the family. But now he was on the other side of the situation. Which brought his thoughts back to what he'd preach at Ed's memorial service.

He bowed his head for a moment, seeking guidance, then pulled the pad toward him and began to write. He started with a portion of Psalm 139, ending with these words: "And in Your Book were all written the days that were ordained for me." That was the passage Ed had used when he broke the news about his problem to the elders. So that was the Scripture Scott would preach at the funeral. He planned to start with Ed's own words: "We are all part of God's master plan. And we all have an expiration date."

Without hesitation, as though the words were flowing directly onto the paper without conscious thought on his part, Scott wrote, "God, and God alone, knows how many days are ordained to each of us. We'd like to argue, to change that number, to have just a bit longer. But we're not privy to that master plan, and so we accept it, knowing that for the believer, death is only a passage from sorrow to joy, from infirmity to wholeness, from the finite to the infinite. And so it was with Ed Farmer. While we envy him that journey, we mourn the void his passing leaves in our lives here on earth."

Abby knew Ed Farmer didn't want to lie in state. "I know some folks will want to make a fuss about me, but just lay me out and bury me. Then get on with your lives," he'd said. She also knew Ed preferred not to be called reverend or pastor. Neither did he use the title of doctor, although he had earned one such degree from the seminary and received two more honorary ones in later years. "I'm just Ed," he'd said. "The man who stands before you in the pulpit is just as human as you. Don't ever put me on a pedestal."

These thoughts ran through Abby's mind as she drove on Tuesday afternoon to the First Congregational Church of Goldman for Ed's service. Although he'd always said he was "just plain Ed," judging by the turnout, a lot of people wanted to honor his memory.

He touched so many lives. And he touched mine.

Although Abby arrived early, she found the sanctuary of the church filling rapidly. Folding chairs had been added to increase the number of people seated in the room to the limit allowed by the local fire code. One of the ushers took her to a vacant seat toward the front of the church. He told her the overflow would be directed to the largest classroom of the building, where they could watch the service via closed-circuit TV on four large sets wheeled in for the purpose.

Abby spent some time in quiet contemplation. Then she opened the printed order of service, but before she could read it, the platform began to fill with the people who would participate in the memorial. One was Associate Pastor Scott Anderson. She'd heard him preach just a few days ago, and he did an admirable job. Abby wondered what this sudden vacancy in the pastorate of the church would mean for Scott. Maybe the identity of the person who delivered the main address would provide a clue.

A closed casket, surrounded by floral arrangements, was situated just below the pulpit. There was a stir followed by the congregation rising as the family entered and was seated.

Then the head of the church's Board of Elders stepped to the podium to make a brief statement. "Ed would be surprised and humbled by the presence of so many assembled here. Many of Ed's friends and colleagues wanted to honor him with their presence today, and his widow has chosen a number to participate throughout the service. They need no introduction other than their names as printed in the program. Rather, we're all here to celebrate the life and legacy of Ed Farmer. So that's what we should do."

One by one, men and women stepped forward and stood behind the lectern. One offered a prayer. Another read one of Ed's favorite Scripture passages. A well-known Gospel singer led the congregation in singing two hymns chosen by the widow. Another rendered a solo. Finally, it was time for the principal message. Abby could hardly contain her surprise when the associate pastor rose and moved to the podium. He opened his Bible, and in a voice filled with emotion, one that broke once or twice, he began to read. *"O, Lord. You have searched me and known me..."*

Bob Bannister reflected that the crowd at the last service at Faith Tabernacle had been smaller and quieter than usual, yet those who did attend seemed pleased at the changes he'd made. Two or three of them lingered after the service to shake his hand and mention how his words had spoken to them. *Why not? I was preaching to myself, and undoubtedly some of the people there had the same needs as I do.* And the changes had been due to Ed Farmer. Then why did he hesitate to attend the memorial service for the man?

Bannister started to leave for the service, each time halting before he got out the door of his house. Would his presence be a distraction? Surely, God wouldn't send a lightning bolt to strike him when he walked in—would He? After all, he'd been there before with no evidence of divine retribution. Did he dare enter the church's doors again? But he wanted to pay his respects to Ed Farmer.

Finally, showing a determination he didn't fully feel, Bannister climbed into his slashed but still drivable car and headed for the First Congregational Church. He wore the same gray suit in which he'd preached at Faith Tabernacle the last two times. He arrived too late to be seated in the crowded sanctuary but followed the directions of the usher to an overflow area.

Bannister took a vacant chair in the almost full classroom, several rows back from one of the closed-circuit TV sets. On the screen, he recognized Scott Anderson standing behind the pulpit, talking about Ed Farmer and his legacy. Several times Scott stopped to wipe unashamed tears from his eyes, and soon Bannister was joining him. He looked around and discovered that he wasn't crying alone. Ed Farmer's death had left behind a hole in the fabric of society. Then Bannister thought of something and smiled through his tears. Ed's life had made a big difference in his own. How big a difference? Time would tell.

Ed liked to lead the Wednesday night prayer meeting, so Scott usually had no official duties at that service. Oh, he shook some hands, greeted those he knew, and made the acquaintance of others, but Ed was in charge. Now Ed Farmer was no longer around, so Scott assumed that, until told differently, he should step in.

Scott flipped through his reference books, thinking about what he was going to say tonight, when someone tapped at his open door. He looked up, expecting it to be one of the secretaries or possibly another staff member, but he was surprised to see Harlan Jones, the chairman of elders, standing there.

"Am I interrupting, Scott?"

"Not at all, Harlan." Scott waved the man in and indicated he should take one of the two chairs opposite his desk. The room was so small that, as Ed used to say, it was necessary to step out into the hall to change your mind. "Sorry about the size of the office. I just didn't feel right using Ed's."

Jones settled his short, stocky frame into one of the chairs. "I understand. That's sort of what I want to talk with you about."

"I realize Ed's death was unexpected," Scott said. "I figured I needed to fill in tonight, unless the elders have already made other arrangements."

"No, that's what we wanted you to do. We appreciate the way you've stepped up. Like a veteran."

If you only knew. "When are you all going to meet to discuss where we go from here? And do you want me there at that meeting?"

Jones leaned back and tapped his chest, apparently reaching for one of the cigars he liked to smoke. But he pulled his hand back, probably realizing he shouldn't smoke in the church building.

"Actually, Scott, we met over breakfast this morning. And we purposely didn't invite you or any of the other church staff. We thought it would help us be more open in our discussion."

Scott nodded. "I understand. So, have you come up with a plan?"

"We have the names of five men who might ... I started to say *replace*, but no one can replace Ed. These are men we think should be considered as our new pastor. We'll share those names with you and the rest of the staff, and pending your agreement, we'll name a committee that will visit with each one and feel them out." He leaned forward in his chair. "The process will probably take several months, because we don't want to move too quickly and make a mistake."

Scott nodded. "And have you thought about men who could fill the pulpit during that time? I know—"

Jones stopped him. "We considered that, and the consensus was that we wanted you to continue to do that for now."

"I ... I don't think you want me. I'm just a rookie."

"As a pastor, maybe, but not as a person. In that regard, you're as mature as any seasoned pastor. You came out of seminary with high recommendations. And what you said from the pulpit, both last Sunday and at Ed's memorial service, convinced the elders that you'll do fine until we find the person to follow him as pastor."

Sometimes Abby attended the Wednesday night service at church, but not tonight. She felt certain this meeting would focus on the hole that Ed Farmer's death left, and that wasn't something she wanted to think about right now. She wanted to talk, but not about the effect on the church. Abby wanted to focus on the consequences of Ed's death on her own life. She couldn't help feeling that it represented a failure on her part.

She'd called her Aunt Kay and asked if she could buy her dinner this evening. "Let me take you out to a nice restaurant. You can relax and let someone else do the cooking *and* wash the dishes."

"You're sweet to ask," Aunt Kay said. "Instead, why don't you come by about six tonight? We'll eat here. It's more comfortable, more private … and I like my own cooking. Besides, I think you want to talk, and we can do it better at my place."

Later that night, Abby sat at Aunt Kay's table, adding butter to a morsel of buttermilk biscuit, before popping it into her mouth. She chewed and swallowed, then sighed contentedly as she dabbed her mouth with a napkin. "Aunt Kay, your cooking is—as always—wonderful."

"Thanks, Hon. One of the joys in my life is cooking for those I love. But are you feeling well? There's still half a piece of chicken fried steak on your plate, and—"

"No, no," Abby said. "If I ate the way you wanted me to, I'd weigh about two hundred pounds. I enjoy your cooking, even though I may leave part of it on my plate."

Kay pushed back from the table and looked at her niece. "You've been awfully quiet tonight."

"Aunt Kay, were you affected by Ed Farmer's death?"

"All the members of the First Congregational Church, including me, were affected. His family will miss him, of course. He was a great preacher. And everyone who knew Ed, even those who never heard him in the pulpit, will miss his smile, his cheerful disposition. So, sure I was affected. Weren't you?"

Abby reached for her iced tea glass, found it empty, and put it down. "Of course."

"You didn't mention his name, but I wondered if he wasn't the one you were talking about the other day. So, you feel a special loss? Why do you think that is? Did he consult you as a physician?"

"No," Abby said. "I wasn't involved in Ed's medical care. Of course, I wish I could have picked up the aneurysm, but I'm okay with that. And Ed was content with the doctors he saw at the medical center. The relationship he sought from me wasn't medical. I was sort of a prayer partner for him."

"He asked you to be his prayer partner? Why's that?"

"He didn't want his wife to worry excessively, so he put on a good face during his experience. But he needed someone he could open up to as he went through it. I had the medical background to understand. And for some reason, now I feel like I've failed him."

Kay scooted her chair closer to her niece. "Did you think you were going to bring him through this with your prayers?"

Abby was silent for a bit. "I guess I was."

"Honey, it's not up to us to tell God what to do. We don't always understand why these things happen. But if it gave Ed comfort to know that you were lifting him up, then you helped him. If you were someone he could talk to, someone who understood the dangers, that was helpful to him. It was what he needed."

"But I wasn't able to effect Dr. Farmer's cure."

"Which is what you really wanted. Right?"

Abby thought about it but was silent. She thought about the saying from the French surgeon that had rolled off her tongue so easily when she was talking to her chief of service. True, in some circumstances, the surgeon dressed the wound, but God healed the patient. When and how He chose to do so wasn't up to her. Was she really trying to take over His role in this case?

Her aunt continued. "If your support was a comfort to Ed, even if you had no ultimate effect on the time and circumstances of his death, you were successful. You had nothing to do with his failure to survive the surgery. We may not be able to answer why while we're here on earth. Meanwhile, all we can do is our best. Actually, that's all God wants of us—whatever we do."

Scott sat in the first row of the church at the start of the Wednesday evening service, listening as Harlan Jones explained to those gathered that the associate pastor would be speaking to them tonight and would fill the pulpit on Sunday as well—for now and the immediate future.

People in attendance asked a few questions about the process of choosing a successor to Ed Farmer, and Harlan answered them. When there were no more questions, he turned to Scott. "I'll let you take it from here."

Scott stood and turned to face the group. "You'll notice that I didn't climb the stairs to the podium. I didn't step behind the pulpit. That's because I want to emphasize that, although I might be directing some services and bringing messages on Sunday morning—and I hope the words will be divinely inspired—the vessel through which they are communicated has the same frailties, the same doubts and fears, the same problems you have." He let his gaze sweep over the assembled people before him.

"Before we get too far into tonight's service, let's take a few moments to pray for Ed Farmer, his family, and all the people who will be affected by his death." *And that includes me.*

The rest of the service went pretty much as usual, with a couple of hymns, a short message, and then time devoted to brief prayers from the congregation. When the service ended, Scott was drenched in sweat, but he felt he'd managed fairly well. He hoped Ed would have approved.

"Dr. Anderson?"

Scott had been shaking hands and greeting the people as they left, and he turned as he heard the voice behind him. He gave a wry smile to Bob Bannister. "No, that title was appropriate when I was practicing medicine, but now I'm just plain Scott."

"Interesting. And because of recent events, I'm no longer Brother Bob. Do you have a few moments to talk in private about where I go from here?"

"Sure," Scott said. *I was wondering the same thing about myself.*

The man consulted his sources and found there was no police activity planned for the area tonight. Unless one of the neighbors started something—which was always a possibility—the action he'd undertake wouldn't be interrupted by the police. He'd done a similar thing before. But this time the conflagration would involve more than Bannister's car.

The neighborhood was quiet, just as one would expect at this time of night. He saw no vehicle traffic, no lights shone, nothing moved. There was a dim streetlight, but that illumination didn't hinder him. Rather, it was just enough to help him accomplish his task. The whole thing would take a couple of minutes at most, and no one would see him.

From his car's trunk, he took two five-gallon cans filled with gasoline. He'd visited two different service stations to fill the containers, storing them in his garage as he prepared for tonight. First, he splashed gasoline onto the porch of the building. Next, he saturated the wooden pillars that held up the roof. What was left in one can, he tossed onto the area around the windows in front of the building. The structure itself probably wouldn't be totally consumed, since there was a great deal of metal and stone used in its construction, but he'd do a lot of damage. There was no doubt in his mind that the contents would catch fire quickly, rendering the building and everything inside unusable.

He took an old towel from his hip pocket and soaked it in the gasoline before placing it on the front steps. For good measure, he emptied the last of the gasoline from the second can on the towel. He took one more look in all directions to confirm that he was totally alone.

"Roast in hell, Bannister," he muttered as he lit the towel with a fireplace lighter and watched the trail of gasoline ignite.

He didn't stay to make certain the flames consumed the building and its contents. He simply hurried to his car, tossed the empty cans into the trunk, started his vehicle, and drove away. By the time he got to the end of the block, he saw a growing red glow in his rearview mirror. He smiled at a job well done.

8

Bob Bannister wasn't certain how long the cell phone that lay on the table at his bedside had been ringing. He slapped the area with his hand until he curled his fingers around it. His eyes only partially open, he brought the phone up to his face and read the Caller ID—Goldman Police Department.

That got Bannister's attention. His first thought was that Randy had been attacked again. His wounds hadn't proven to be life-threatening, and his status was stable enough that he'd been discharged from the hospital this morning. Surely, something else hadn't happened to him. Or had it? Was that why the police were calling?

Bannister answered the call just before it rolled over to voice mail. "Hello," he managed to croak.

"Mr. Bannister, this is Sergeant Kirkham of the Goldman Police. Are you the owner of the Faith Tabernacle?"

Bannister shook his fuzzy head and tried to gather his senses. Finally, he swung his feet over and sat on the side of the bed. "Would you repeat that?"

"Are you the owner of Faith Tabernacle? You know, the building that used to be an Albertson's before they moved out."

"I ... I hold services there, but I don't own it." He stopped to think as the fog cleared from his sleep-addled brain. "I guess ... You know, I don't really know who owns that building. Jase Miller is the one who offered me the use of it since it was standing vacant. I guess you could call him."

"So, it's not your building?"

"No, that's what I just tried to say." Bannister pulled the blanket from the bed and arranged it around his shoulders. His eyes lit on the chair near the bed, and he headed for it.

"Would you have a night watchman or janitor or anyone staying there?"

Bannister thought of Randy. Surely, he didn't stay at the Faith Tabernacle overnight. Right now, he should be asleep in his apartment. "I ... No, we don't have anyone like that. Why?" He sat down, which was a good thing, considering the sergeant's next words.

"There was a fire there tonight. The fire department came out, but the building was fully engulfed by the time they got there. The contents are probably a total loss. What we're trying to do now is identify the body we found in one of the rooms."

"Here's the patient list for this morning."

Abby looked at the sheet of paper her secretary Ruby placed on her desk. "Anything unusual?"

"Not really." She waved a handful of pink phone message slips. "We got these from the answering service, but they're all pretty routine. Gloria and I will handle them."

Abby smiled and took a sip from the cup on her desk. "Sounds like you don't even need me. Maybe I'll just stay in my office and drink coffee this morning."

"In your dreams," Ruby said, laughing over her shoulder as she headed back to the front office next to the waiting room.

Her receptionist had been gone about five minutes when the intercom on Abby's desk sounded. "Yes?"

"Doctor Anderson is on line one. He wants to speak with you."

Abby couldn't recall a physician in the community with the last name Anderson. Then it came to her. Ruby meant Scott Anderson. The associate pastor must have used his title to get past the receptionist. "I'll talk with him. Let me know when my first patient is in the room."

She punched the blinking button. "This is Dr. Davis. Is this call medical or theological?"

"I guess it's theological," Scott said. "Sorry for playing the doctor card, but I really need to talk with you."

"I understand. So, how can I help?"

"Is there any way I can see you around noon today?"

Abby frowned. This was the same way Ed Farmer had approached her. Was there something about the pastorate of that church that caused people to call her? "I should be through with my patients about noon. Want to come by at that time?"

"Sounds fine."

"Is this something—"

"We'll talk about it when I see you," Scott said, hanging up on her.

Gloria tapped on the door. "Your first patient is here." She started to turn away, but swiveled her head around to ask, "Did Dr. Anderson have a problem?"

"I don't know," Abby said. "I really don't know."

Bob Bannister felt a chill, but it wasn't just the cold air in the morgue. Once Sergeant Kirkham told him about the body found in the burned-out building, he knew that he'd have to help the police in their efforts to identify the remains. And that meant a trip to the morgue, something he didn't look forward to. If the body were Randy's—and Bannister thought it likely was—then there'd be the question of notifying his next of kin, arranging the memorial service, and deciding... No, he didn't want to go there. Not yet.

Sergeant Kirkham had handed Bannister a blue paper gown and a surgical mask. "You'll want to put these on. Burned bodies... well, they can sometimes generate a smell you have trouble getting off your clothes. Or out of your nostrils."

Soon the sergeant, his uniform covered by an identical gown, stood beside Bannister, one hand on his elbow as though to prevent his running away. Probably a good thing. He had been tempted a couple of times to turn around and exit the building rather than going through with this job.

The morgue attendant, wearing a dark blue scrub suit and a surgical cap, wheeled a covered gurney into the room, stopping next to the two men. Bannister noticed he wasn't wearing a mask. Did people get used to it after a time? He wasn't certain whether he smelled something, or it was just his imagination. In either case, he wanted to get this over with.

The police sergeant tightened his grip on Bannister's arm. "If you feel faint, take some deep breaths. If that doesn't help, sit over there, bend over, and put your head between your knees."

Bannister looked behind him and located the chair sitting against the wall. He hoped he wouldn't need it, but it was nice to know it was there. "Thanks."

"Are you ready?" asked the policeman.

He swallowed hard and nodded. His throat was too dry for him to speak.

The sergeant stepped forward, and he and the morgue attendant pulled the sheet down just far enough to uncover the head and neck region of the corpse.

"The post-mortem exam showed he died of smoke inhalation, which is why you don't see any burns in this region," the attendant said. "That's not the case further down, but all you need to see is his face."

The corpse appeared composed, almost peaceful. Just at the top edge of the sheet Bannister could see the beginning of the heavy, black-silk sutures used to close the Y-shaped incision of the autopsy. The scalp closure stitching was partially hidden by the long gray hair that covered the man's head.

"Take a good look," Sergeant Kirkham said.

Taking a deep breath and half closing his eyes, Bannister focused his attention on the body lying on the gurney. He looked for almost a minute before he turned away.

"Well, do you recognize him," the sergeant asked.

"Yes." Bannister didn't realize he'd been holding his breath until this moment, when he let out all the air in his lungs in a faint sigh. He knew his heart hadn't really stopped beating, but now he felt it as his pulse sounded in his ears. He swallowed twice before he spoke. "That's a man who attended our services quite a few times. I'm sorry, but I don't know his name."

But thank God it's not Randy.

"My nurse will be in shortly to set up your lab work," Abby said. "Call me in the meantime if you have any questions or problems. Otherwise, I'll contact you when I have the results, and we'll make a decision about how to proceed." She walked out of the exam room and looked expectantly at Gloria. "Where to next?"

"That's your last patient for this morning," her nurse said. "And I've moved those who are scheduled for this afternoon as you requested. You're free for the rest of the day." She hesitated. "Do we need to do anything about your patients scheduled for tomorrow?"

"No," Abby said. "At least, I don't think so."

It was obvious from Gloria's expression that she would like to know what was going on, but she didn't ask further. Instead, she shrugged. "Dr. Anderson's waiting in your office."

"Okay. When you get Ms. Turner's lab work and return appointment set up, you and Ruby can check out and go to lunch."

"Uh, would you like me to hang around?"

It took Abby a moment to figure out what her nurse was asking. "I think I'm safe being left alone with a man of the cloth. But thanks anyway."

As Abby moved toward her office, she couldn't help feeling a bit of *déjà vu,* remembering how Ed Farmer had sat in her office just a week ago. Now the man who was temporarily taking Ed's place waited in her office, wanting ... what?

Scott rose from one of the client chairs when Abby walked into her office. "I appreciate your seeing me like this."

Abby motioned him back to his seat and took the chair behind her desk. "No problem. But you said it's nothing medical. I'll have to admit I'm not the most active member of your congregation, so I doubt that it has to do with church business. I don't know what else we might have to discuss. Want to clue me in?"

Scott leaned forward in his chair, betraying his ill-at-ease feeling through his posture. "I suppose you'd call this an identity crisis. It has to do with my profession... whatever that turns out to be."

Abby wasn't comfortable with the direction the conversation was going, so she tried to head it off. "I'm not a counselor. But I can refer you to someone."

Scott shook his head. "I wanted to talk with you because—like me—you're a physician. And although you say you're not very active in the church, what I've seen of your actions tells me you're a believer. So, I think you're the right person for me to talk with."

"Look, Dr. Anderson—"

"Please, it's Scott." He turned his head to look at the closed office door. "Maybe you need to know why I left medicine in the first place."

Abby wanted to look at her watch. She thought about what she had planned for the afternoon, but she sensed her visit with Scott was important. There was time. "Suppose you tell me."

"You know how doctors are—at least I was. We think we should be able to cure anything. And the corollary to that is we get sort of peeved at people with vague, probably insignificant complaints."

Abby nodded. "I try not to do that, but I know you're not the first doctor to whom that's happened."

"Well, my wife kept mentioning vague complaints. I told her it was probably nothing."

"Did you do a real history? And I'm betting you didn't do an examination. Right?"

Scott shook his head. "No, I thought I could tell she was okay. I mean, a doctor's wife. She couldn't have anything really wrong, could she?" He took a shuddering breath. "But eventually, she went to her primary care doctor, who did take a history. Then she did an exam. After that she sent Erica to a specialist, who did some tests, performed a more thorough exam, and diagnosed late-stage carcinoma of the ovary."

Abby started to reach out to Scott, but at the last minute she pulled back. No, he didn't need sympathy for his loss. He was looking for absolution from another professional. But could she give it? She'd try.

"Scott, the symptoms of ovarian malignancy are usually non-specific. The only way that disease can be diagnosed is with a high index of suspicion followed by a thorough exam, including a pelvic."

"So why didn't I pay attention to her? Why didn't I... Oh, why?"

"You know, don't you, that doctors miss this diagnosis all the time? And your wife really wasn't your patient."

He looked away. "But she was my wife. I was a general surgeon, and a good one. I thought I could diagnose her problem just by listening to her complaints. I was too confident... and it cost me the woman I loved."

"I suspect that your wife—"

"Erica."

"I suspect Erica told you several times after the diagnosis was made that it wasn't your fault," Abby said. "As a physician, you know that 80 percent of these cases aren't diagnosed until they're beyond surgery."

"But I'm a doctor! My wife should be in that 20 percent." He leaned back in his chair and breathed heavily. Finally, he said in a quiet voice, "After she died, I couldn't go back to the hospital. How about that? A surgeon who couldn't stand to be in a hospital. I took time away from my practice, but there was nothing to do at home but grieve and think about what I couldn't change."

"So..."

"So, I decided to quit medicine. I convinced myself that maybe God wanted me to follow through on the brief time I was a teen and thought He was calling me. I found that I had enough college credits to get into seminary. I applied and was accepted."

"A rebound reaction? A sort of penance?"

Scott nodded. "I guess, but once I was accepted, I decided to go through with it. I'll admit that I went through the first several months at seminary in a fog, but I eventually got interested. I studied, asked questions of the faculty, read a lot, and by the last year I guess I caught the eye of my professors. But now that I have to stand in the pulpit, I don't know if I have the depth to carry it out."

"And you want my support in going forward?"

"No," Scott said. "I want to know what you think about my going back into medicine."

The blinds were closed in Bannister's house, even though it was noonday bright outside. Several times he looked at the bottle of whiskey that sat on his kitchen table, and once he actually reached for it. But he brought his hand back empty.

If anything called for some Dutch courage, a trip to the morgue did. But he'd resisted. At last Bannister rose, looked regretfully at the bottle, and placed it at the back of the cupboard. He'd thought about getting rid of it completely, pouring it out, but he wasn't there yet. A small part of him thought he might eventually need it.

He sank into a kitchen chair and cradled his head in his hands. Of course, when the policeman had told him of the corpse in the burnt building, he feared the man who was killed by the fire was Randy. But it wasn't.

The corpse was that of a man who'd been at some of the services. No, it wasn't Randy, and he had heaved a sigh of relief when he made that discovery. But he recognized the older man and felt a new and unusual emotion surging through him—sorrow at the death of someone who had heard him preach. He wasn't sure he'd ever experienced that emotion before.

At the time he first saw him, Bannister had thought the victim was attending services because he was seeking a closer relationship with God. Now it dawned on him that it was more likely he was searching for a place to sleep where he wouldn't be disturbed. Probably the older man had nosed around in the Tabernacle to find a spot for himself to use at night. And now he was dead.

Although Bannister had never been there, his … What could he call Randy? His helper, his sidekick? Once, Randy had told him he had a furnished room near the building that housed the Faith Tabernacle. Apparently, that was where he went after leaving the hospital. The truth was, Bannister had been putting off checking up on Randy. Maybe he should go now. Or maybe he could delay it for a little while longer.

His visit to the morgue hadn't sharpened his appetite, but Bannister knew he should eat something. He rose from the chair and was looking through the store of canned goods in his pantry when his phone rang. Who could be calling? It was probably about the fire. Or perhaps it was Randy, finally checking in.

"Hello."

"Is this Brother Bob Bannister?"

"Actually, just Bob will do." Bannister's brow wrinkled with the question that ran through his mind. It was a woman's voice on the other end of the call. He knew very few women in town and couldn't think why any of them would be calling him. "Who's this?"

"My name won't mean anything to you," she said. "Call me Lois. I'm the woman you healed at the service almost two weeks ago."

Bannister eased into a chair. He'd worried about this call for the past ten days. Now it had come. Was this woman an investigative reporter? Was she calling for comments before her story appeared in print or as a TV special? Could he convince her he'd changed? He worked to keep his voice steady. "How can I help you?"

"I'm sure that by now you've figured out I bribed one of your ushers to let me take the place of the woman you were going to 'heal' that night. And I suspect you know what I planned to do afterward." There was a pause. "But before you got to the healing, you said some things that touched my heart. After I went down that aisle and out of the building, I was ready to write a story about your fake faith-healing. But, when I sat down at my computer, I couldn't do it."

"I don't understand."

"I found that I was changed. Although I had material that would make a good story, I couldn't write it. It just didn't seem right to hurt you after hearing some of the things you said. You literally turned around my life."

"I'm glad. But—"

"My boss kept after me to do the story I was sent to write, but it just wouldn't come. Inside the show you put on was a kernel of truth. And for some reason, I found that kernel. I found the Gospel. And it changed me."

Bannister couldn't believe it. "You mean—?"

"I left that job. Actually, I've left the area. At the time, I worked out of Dallas and came to Goldman to do my story. Now I have a position in Houston, one that doesn't involve writing stories that are sensational. I ... I just wanted you to know how you changed my life." Her voice caught as she added the next statement. "I understand you've altered the services. Now you focus on preaching. I'm glad."

Bannister started to say something, but the woman had already hung up. He put the phone down, and Ed Farmer's words came back to ring in his ears. "God may have something in mind. Ask Him to show you what it is." *Maybe He just did.*

9

Scott looked at his watch and saw he'd occupied all of Abby's time during her lunch hour. "Let me buy you lunch."

She balked, but he insisted. Finally, Abby gave in. "But I'll have to leave in about an hour. I have an appointment."

Now the two of them sat in one of the back booths at RJ's. They had been served their food—a cheeseburger for Scott, a small salad for Abby—but they seemed more interested in talking than eating. At least Scott was. Abby was definitely preoccupied.

Scott looked around to make certain no one was within eavesdropping distance. "I've told you about my problems. Why don't you tell me yours?"

Abby almost bristled. "What makes you think I have any?"

"You're trying to give me your attention, but I can see something is on your mind. Want to tell me?"

"No ... No, let's focus on your problems."

"Okay," Scott said. "Maybe if you point out some of the difficulties that go along with being a family practitioner in a less-than-metropolitan area like this, it will help me make my decision."

Abby's salad sat forgotten. "Maybe you're talking to the wrong person. You know a bit about medical practice, but you haven't been a member of the clergy long enough to make a valid comparison."

"I guess you're right. There are some negatives to either profession."

Abby paused to drink some water. "And don't think that you'll get away from the problems of the people—either congregants or patients—especially in a small town. If you're considering a move, I can tell you that going from the ministry back into medicine is tantamount to jumping from the frying pan into the fire."

"Are you saying—"

"Any clergyman can tell you about what you give up as a minister. They'll have a lot to say." Abby looked fully in his eyes. "But it's the same whether you're in the medical field or religion. Doctors may tend to rashes and sprained ankles, but more often than not, they end up counseling people. At least, I do. Matter of fact, that may be the toughest part of the job if the physician lives out his or her beliefs."

"So, what you're saying…"

"What you're doing right now is similar to what I do. It probably was different being a surgeon, but I'll bet you did a lot of the counseling I'm talking about. Didn't you have people whose problems weighed you down? And how did you feel if they had a fatal prognosis? What's the difference in standing by the bedside of a dying person, whether you're their doctor or their pastor?"

Scott nodded. He shoved his partially eaten cheese-burger aside. "I think what you're saying is that changing professions, whether going back to medicine or getting into teaching or even training to be an accountant—none of that is going to help what I feel."

"Not if your problem is letting go of the guilt you feel about your wife's death," she said. "If that's the case, I suggest you change your attitude, not your occupation."

It wasn't that Bannister couldn't move. It was more a case of not really wanting to. He might never get up from the chair in his living room. What was the opposite of "galvanized?" He thought about checking the dictionary he kept with his other books, but decided it was too much trouble.

Was he discouraged? No, that didn't fully describe the way he felt. Disheartened? Maybe, but by what? By the opposition that had manifested itself in acts such as damaging his car? Or was it the cuts and bruises Randy had sustained from an attacker? How about the fire that destroyed the building he'd been using? What about the man who had died in that fire? Were these the triggering forces?

No, what was going on inside him was more than the result of these malicious attacks. What was really upsetting him was the change that he faced, a change that meant recognizing and embracing what he'd tried to ignore for years. It was putting aside the showmanship and grasping an unfamiliar concept—faith. And he wasn't certain he was ready to move away from what had become familiar, even if he felt himself being led in that direction every day.

Bannister heard a faint knocking at his door. He hadn't done a lot to hide his address. It obviously had been easy enough to find for whoever slipped those notes under his door, or pinned them there with a knife, or damaged his car, or assaulted Randy. Had they come back to finish the job? And if they did, would he care?

He continued to sit. Maybe if he ignored whoever was at the door, they'd go away. But they didn't. In a moment, he heard it again. Tap, tap.

When he finally got up and moved slowly toward the door, Bannister initially wished he had a gun. Then again, he wondered if he'd use it. Probably not.

Through the spy hole in the door, he saw Randy standing on the porch, looking around and checking over his shoulder, jittering as he waited for the door to open. The bandages on his arms and neck were dirty, the tape coming loose in places. Had he changed them since he left the hospital? Those pieces of gauze were silent reminders to Bannister that whoever had done this was playing for keeps. Despite the warmth inside the house, a shiver ran up his spine.

He opened the door. "Randy, are you okay?" He stepped back and gestured. "Come inside."

Once the door closed behind him, Randy said, "I don't want anyone to see me."

Bannister led him into the front room. The drawn drapes drew Randy's approving nod. He chose one of the two chairs in the room, turning it slightly so that he faced his boss in the other one.

"I've been worried about you, Randy," Bannister said. "I tried to contact you after you left the hospital, but there was no answer when I called your cell phone." He decided not to mention his latest call, when he was afraid Randy had perished in the fire.

"I've moved around," Randy said. "Actually, I guess you could say I've been in hiding."

"Hiding from what?"

"Not what … but who. I thought the person who slashed your car—and me—might make another attempt on my life. Then last night I saw …" Randy looked around. "You sure we're safe here?"

"The door is locked. The drapes are drawn. Now go on."

"I've made it a habit to walk around the Faith Tabernacle building every night, checking things out, making sure all the doors were locked and stuff. I kept this up after you … after you changed the services around. Of course, I didn't do that while I was in the hospital, but I started again after I was discharged."

"And you saw something you shouldn't have?"

"I saw what happened at the building the night of the fire." He looked around the room again. Then he said in a quieter voice, "I saw someone set the fire. And I can identify him."

"But you told the police—"

Randy put his finger to his lips. "Not so loud. I saw the man who set the fire. And I'm pretty sure it was the same one who slashed your car and cut me."

"Have you told the police about this?"

"You know how I feel about the police. I finally got up the nerve to come and tell you about it. I figured you can decide what to do."

"Aunt Kay, the food was delicious, as always," Abby said. "And it feels so good to be here."

"I'm glad to have you here." The older woman bustled around the kitchen, cleaning up the supper dishes. She looked at Abby's almost full plate before scraping off the food into the disposal. "I wish you could be here more. Of course, it would also be nicer if you ate more of my cooking while you were here. You used to enjoy it."

"I still do. It's just ..." Abby moved behind her aunt and gave her a hug. "That's what I want to talk about with you."

"Of course." Kay dried her hands on her apron. "Let's go in the living room. Those dishes can wait."

In a moment, both women were seated, Kay in the overstuffed chair, Abby on the sofa at right angles to it. "Now, what do you have to tell me?" the older woman asked.

"I had an appointment this afternoon with a doctor in Dallas."

"Who did you see?"

"The name won't mean anything to you," Abby said. "You'd been teasing me because I haven't been eating well when I come over here, but I've sort of blown you off. Then I developed some vague abdominal complaints, and after that I noticed some other problems. Bottom line, I finally decided to get that checkup I've been putting off."

"I'm glad you did," Kay said. "Did they find anything?"

Abby nodded. "I didn't want anyone around here to know, so I saw Dr. Adams at the medical center about two weeks ago. My symptoms were pretty nondescript, and on a routine PE he didn't find anything disturbing. He ordered some routine lab tests, but in addition, he got a CA 125."

"What's that?" Kay asked.

"It's an antigen that's often elevated in cancer patients, especially females, and mine was high. Dr. Adams ordered some more tests, and some of them were abnormal. Today

I had an appointment with the gynecologist he sent me to see, Dr. Pritchard."

Kay frowned. "This is beginning to sound bad."

"It probably is," Abby replied. "Dr. Pritchard confirmed the presence of a mass on my ovary. Maybe both of them. She feels it's a strong possibility I have ovarian cancer."

Kay's hand flew to her mouth. "Oh my. What's the outlook for that? What's the treatment? What—"

"That's the problem, Aunt Kay. At first the patient thinks the same way I did—these are just minor problems and eventually they'll go away. But they keep hanging on. And once these nondescript symptoms are significant enough to send the patient to the doctor, the prognosis may not be good."

"But it's not hopeless, is it? You're going to fight this, aren't you?"

"Of course, I'll fight. No one's ever accused me of being a quitter. Dr. Pritchard will perform a laparoscopy. If the biopsy and frozen section confirm her diagnosis, she'll do a surgical resection—ovaries, tubes, maybe the uterus. Depends on what she finds. But I'd prefer a complete hysterectomy. Depending on what stage it is, I'll go through chemotherapy or radiation, maybe both."

"So you'll never have children? I know you've always wanted to get married and have kids."

"I look at it this way, Aunt Kay. I can't have any children—even by adoption—if I'm dead. My first priority is to lick this thing."

"Absolutely, and while the doctors are doing what they do best, I'll do what I do best. I'll support you with prayer, just the way you did for Ed Farmer."

It was one of those early fall Texas days when, despite the predictions of the weather forecasters, it decided to rain. The rain came down in sudden torrents, making it a perfect Saturday to stay inside, drink coffee, and think long thoughts. In the case of Scott Anderson, those thoughts included meditating about the sermon he'd preach tomorrow.

The ringing of the phone made him put down his coffee cup and pull his cell from his pocket. He looked at the display and discovered the call was from Abby.

"Scott Anderson."

"Scott, this is Abby Davis. Did I interrupt something important?"

He discovered the coffee cup he was holding was almost empty. And this might be a long conversation. "Not really, but could you hold for just a moment?"

He refilled his cup, then he settled into the chair he'd occupied when she called. "Now I'm set, Abby. How can I help you?"

"You know how yesterday you finally told me why you left the practice of medicine? Why you blamed yourself for not diagnosing your wife's carcinoma of the ovary earlier? Remember that?"

Scott's gut tightened. He'd had enough trouble telling Abby about this yesterday. Why was she bringing it up again today? "Yes," he answered through tight lips.

"Well, you'll appreciate the irony in this story."

He listened to her recital, complete with medical details, but, contrary to Abby's words, he didn't appreciate the irony at all. Scott knew the road that was ahead of Abby, and the likelihood that, despite all the measures known to modern medicine, she might not survive. "I'm so sorry to hear all this."

"It's quite a shock, and I'm still trying to take it in. But notice that it was diagnosed because my doctor ordered a lab test that came back abnormal—not because of anything he could see. I'd suggest you stop beating yourself up about not diagnosing your wife's tumor."

"I guess you're right." He hesitated before uttering his next words. "My brain realizes that. I hope someday my heart will too."

"So do I," Abby said. "I just wanted you to know."

"What can I do for you now?"

"Nothing. I'll let my office staff know about this tomorrow. Then I plan to call around to the doctors in Goldman and make certain my patients are taken care of." Abby paused, as though to give emphasis to the next part. "I'd appreciate it if you didn't say anything at church about this yet. Let me tell it my way."

"Of course. But after the word gets out, can we add you to the church's prayer list?"

"I suppose that's really why I called," Abby said. "I'm pretty certain, after our conversation yesterday, that you know the emotional upheaval I'm going through right now."

Scott recalled the highs and lows both he and Erica experienced after her diagnosis was made. "Yes. Yes, I do."

"I assured you yesterday that I'd pray for you as you consider your decision. Well, 'turn about is fair play,' as the saying goes. Will you pray for me ... please?"

Bob Bannister was about to call Randy and tell him he was ready to pull the plug on everything. But before he could carry that through, his phone rang.

"Bob, this is Scott Anderson. I wanted to see if this offer would help you."

What offer? Was Anderson ready to provide some sort of support? Was the church? No, surely the members of the First Congregational Church would be happy to see this splinter group dispersed. "What is it?"

"I discussed the fire damage to your building with our elders. I have to say that initially they weren't thrilled with the concept I proposed, but I eventually sold them on it. We'd like to offer one of our largest classrooms to you for services one night a week. Of course, it's not as big as what you had in the building that burned, and we probably couldn't fit in your musicians, but—"

"Actually, most of my musicians have already left, seeking employment elsewhere. Of the paid staff, only Randy and I are left. And I was about to let him know that I'm ready to shut down my operation here."

"Look. I know how Ed's advice affected you. He affected a lot of us. But since you changed your services, the preaching you've done has been good, especially for someone with no seminary background. How about getting the word out that you'll be meeting here on Saturdays? Your preaching is especially good for people seeking to know more about God."

"I . . . I don't know what to say."

"You may not last long here, but at least when you quit it will be your decision, not because of that person who tried to burn you out."

"Thanks, Scott. I'll try not to disappoint you." Bannister clicked off the phone.

At least this gives me one more chance to do things the right way.

Bannister figured it would be hard for him to get through the service in these new surroundings. But once he hit his stride, the message he delivered in the classroom of the First Congregational Church seemed to flow freely, and he didn't think anyone noticed his initial nervousness.

As he preached that Saturday night, his eyes swept over the people sitting before him. Although the numbers were smaller than at the Faith Tabernacle, a lot of the people who'd been attending his services showed up here. Most of them were actually those who'd started coming after he moved from what Ed had called "entertainment" to straight Biblical preaching. Bannister hoped they'd come back for more.

When the service ended, a few of the congregation came up to shake his hand and compliment him on the message. "Just preaching to myself," was his usual reply. One older man seemed to linger at the back of the room while it emptied. His dress shirt was clean, although slightly wrinkled, his tie a bit wider than currently fashionable. His dark suit stood in contrast with the casual dress of most of the crowd.

The man didn't talk to anyone, and Bannister wondered if he was waiting to see him. But when everyone had finally exited, the stranger had left. Probably someone who wanted to talk but changed his mind at the last minute. Bannister had encountered that before.

In the small room nearby that Scott had told him to use as his unofficial "office," Bannister shed his suit coat and loosened his tie. Habit made him look for the bottle and glass he usually kept close at hand, so he could pour a drink to help him come down from the natural high of the service. But that bottle was in a closed cupboard in his apartment, a visible reminder of the changes he had made—both in his service and his life.

It all stems from the advice you gave me, Ed Farmer.

He gave a nod in an imaginary toast to the deceased pastor.

Bannister wished he could have convinced Randy to go to the police with information about the person who'd been opposing him. But despite telling him about it, Randy didn't want to go to the authorities. "It's just my word against his. And can you guess who they'd believe? I'm a parolee—actually, I'm a parole-breaker. No, I can't do it."

They'd have to figure out another way. Meanwhile, Bannister also had to reach a decision about what he was going to do, and how to go about it.

A tap at the door of the room was so faint he wasn't sure he actually heard it.

"Yes?"

Randy poked his face through the aperture of the partially opened door and looked around. Then he slipped into the room and closed the door behind him. "Good service Brother … Mr. Bannister."

Randy had apparently attempted to clean up before the evening's service. He wore a clean T-shirt and his jeans had no holes in the knees. He had changed the bandages on his arms and neck, and the new ones fairly gleamed they were so white.

"Thanks, Randy." Bannister gestured to the chair on the other side of the desk from him. "I didn't see you in there during the service."

"I … I was in an adjoining classroom. I could hear through the partially open door, but no one could see me." He directed a furtive look toward the door. "Did he show up?"

"I don't know. Remember, I've never seen the man," Bannister said. "All I have is your description."

A noise at the back of the room caused Bannister to look up. In contrast to Randy's hesitant entrance, the man who came in was bold about it. This was the man who lingered at the back of the room after the service. At the time, Bannister had thought that perhaps he wanted to talk about the state of his soul. But the gun in his hand indicated he was more interested in getting rid of the two men who sat before him.

10

While much of Goldman was doing whatever they did on a Saturday night—having dinner out with friends, enjoying a movie, sitting at home in front of the TV, cheering their local high school football team—Scott Anderson sat at the table that served as a desk in his small apartment. Books lay scattered over the surface, some with pieces of yellow paper marking the pages that held pertinent information. Scott had his eyes closed, searching for the thought that he'd just had, one that now eluded him when he went to write it down.

He realized the sermon he'd preach tomorrow morning could very well set the tone for the future of the First Congregational Church of Goldman. Like any church, there were probably a certain number of the congregation who'd leave after Ed's death. Scott hoped to convey the important message that the real center of the church wasn't the pastor.

Scott wondered if he should also reveal the unrest in his mind, the quandary with which he continued to battle. If he left the church while they were still seeking a replacement for Ed Farmer, would that contribute further to its decline? And should that even factor into his decision? Or should he base his actions solely on what was best for him?

In the midst of all this, he thought of Bob Bannister. Here was another man faced with a change in the direction of his life. For some reason, Scott felt led to pray for Bannister right then. He didn't know why, but he'd learned that these urges couldn't be explained by logic. No, Bannister was—to use an expression he'd heard before— "on his heart."

"What do you want?" Bannister said to the man who approached his desk. The stranger appeared to be about sixty years old. As he walked closer, Bannister recoiled at the strange gleam in the man's eyes—a gleam he'd seen only once before, in someone who began raving during the services of the tent evangelist with whom he'd spent a couple of years as an apprentice.

"I tried to warn you away," the man said. "I sent you notes. I destroyed your car. I burned your building. But you're like a Phoenix that continues to rise from its ashes. You won't die. And you keep poisoning the people of this area."

So that's who this is—the guy Randy saw setting fire to our building.

"Hang on." Bannister held up his open palm. "If you've been watching me, you know things aren't the same as they were. I'll admit that when I came to this city, I focused more on entertainment than anything else in my services, but that's changed."

"And you could just as easily change back," the man said.

Bannister was no expert, but he thought the gun the man held looked like an automatic of some sort. He didn't know if the pistol had a safety, or if it was off or on. But the finger inside the trigger guard meant the man was serious about shooting him. And the bullets fired from that gun could kill him in an instant.

During the confrontation, Randy stood, transfixed, along the back wall of the room. Now he inched toward the door but stopped when the man wheeled and pointed the gun at him.

"Hold it right there!" He motioned toward the front of the room where Bannister had come to his feet. "Move over closer to him. I was wondering if you were in the service, but I didn't see you. Now this lets me kill two birds with one stone, or, perhaps I should say, with two bullets."

"Why are you doing this?" Bannister asked.

The man's expression didn't change, although the light in his eyes seemed to grow even brighter. "When you first brought your act to Goldman, I knew you were a phony putting on a big act. I saw you for what you were. Most people who were real believers dismissed you. But I could see that some people could be drawn away from our churches by what you were offering. And the Bible warns us to beware of people like you—people who prowl like a lion in the night.

"But I've changed," Bannister said. "This evening you could see how I've redone the services. I may even shut down services completely if I can figure out how best to do it. I'll encourage attendees to get right with God and align with some of the other churches you're talking about."

The man shook his head. "Words and promises—not worth anything. The only way to get rid of what you're offering is to get rid of you." He gestured to Randy. "Closer. Stand next to him. That way, you can both enter into hell at the same time."

The man stood about ten feet from Bannister and Randy. Did that mean one of them could jump him? If so, would he shoot the other one? Whatever they were going to do, it would have to be done soon.

Then a strange voice made the man turn his head for a fraction of a second. "I had a feeling that I should come by here and see how things went," Scott Anderson said. Then he apparently saw the gun. "What—"

Bannister prepared to dive for the man's gun hand, but before he could move Randy grabbed a folding chair and sailed it at the gunman's head, knocking him to the floor, facedown. Even in his dazed condition, the stranger held onto the gun, but a strong kick from Randy sent it flying. Then he straddled the dazed gunman, pinning his arms behind his back while calmly looking up at Bannister.

"Pick up his gun and cover him. If he tries to get up, shoot him—I'd suggest in the right shoulder. That will put him out of commission for a while."

Bannister's hand shook, but he did as he was told.

"Come up here," Randy called to Scott. "Take the laces out of his shoes and lash his thumbs together, tight. Then use his belt to restrain his ankles."

The man under Randy started to recover. He raised his head and said, "You can't—"

"We can and we did," Randy said. Then he turned to his boss, who still held the gun on the man on the floor. "I guess that's one advantage of the life I used to live. I learned never to wait for the other guy to make the first move. Act when there's an opening and use whatever weapon's handy."

"I've secured him," Scott said. He stood up and pulled out his cell phone. "Now I'll call the police."

Randy frowned. "Let me leave before they get here."

"No," Bannister said. "Your testimony will be critical in convicting the man."

Randy started to get up. "No, I—."

"Please, Randy."

Slowly, Randy nodded. "I'll trust you, Brother... Mr. Bannister."

Scott dialed 9-1-1 and asked the dispatcher to send patrolmen to the church's educational building, explaining that he and two other men were holding a gunman there.

Randy looked down at the assailant, who now lay restrained on the floor. "Did you search him to make certain he didn't have any other weapons?"

"I'm afraid I didn't," Scott said.

"Just in case..." Randy came up empty in his search until he came to the man's coat pocket. He reached in and pulled out a surgeon's scalpel wrapped in a piece of paper.

"I guess that was in case the gun wasn't the right tool for what he had in mind," Bannister said.

Randy nodded. "That's the funny-looking knife he used on your car—and to cut me."

As he was putting his cell phone away, Scott turned to Bannister. "Do you know who this man is?"

"No, I saw him for the first time tonight."

"I've only been in Goldman for a short time, but I recognize him. It's Dr. Carlton Willis. I've even heard Dr. Abby Davis talking about him. But somehow I think his days of practicing medicine in this community are over."

On Sunday evening, Abby sat back in her chair in Aunt Kay's living room. "Well, tomorrow I'll have my surgery."

Kay settled into her recliner and put up her feet. "And you'll come through it fine."

"I hope so. I keep thinking back to what Ed Farmer told me. Do everything you can, then turn it over to God. That's what I'm ready to do."

"Good advice." Kay leaned toward her niece. "I've looked this up on Google. Since you're under sixty-five, your chances of a cure are better."

Abby smiled. "You really have been looking into this, although I'd warn you against believing everything you read on the Internet."

Kay held up her hand. "I know. But these statistics are from a reliable site."

"Fine, but I'm not as interested in statistics as I am in results."

"Have you lined up other doctors to care for your patients while you're fighting this?"

"I've called several of my colleagues to see if they'll handle my patients until I'm well enough to practice again. Dr. Willis can't take care of his cancer patients now, so this may throw a double load on some of them, but I think it will work out all right."

"Sounds like you've done all you can." Kay hitched her chair a bit closer. "Now it's time to turn it over to God."

With the blinds closed and the drapes drawn over the windows, Bob Bannister's house was dark inside. But that was the way he wanted it today. As he sat in his living room on Monday morning, he didn't want even a single ray of sunshine to illuminate the room. He wanted to ponder the situation. And darkness was the proper setting for it.

True, with the capture of Dr. Carlton Willis, the driving force opposing him in Goldman had been neutralized. On the other hand, fire had destroyed the building where he'd been holding services.

His musicians had scattered. No one knew where the few people who served as ushers had gone. Other than Randy, his whole group had deserted him. Vaguely, he tried to recall Bible stories about situations where it seemed that everyone had abandoned the central character of the story. What did they do? What should he do?

Since there had been a change, not just in his preaching but in his life, Bannister honestly didn't know what the future held. He couldn't hold the kind of services he used to—even if his people hadn't already left. If he left, the remnant that remained would either find a church or drift away from organized religion. Was he responsible for the latter group? Should he stay and minister to those few? If he did, he'd have to find some sort of job to support himself.

In response to a knock, Bannister rose and moved slowly toward the front door. He looked through the peephole and saw Randy, standing on his doorstep, smiling. He unlocked the door, undid the chain, and beckoned him in. "Come in, Randy. Have a seat."

As Randy took a chair, Bannister said, "Since Dr. Willis isn't in a position to do anything about your presence here, why don't we let in a little light?" After a confirming nod from Randy, he opened the drapes and adjusted the blinds to let in the light from outside. "How did your session with the police go?"

"Better than I might have imagined," Randy said. "I decided to be up-front with the detectives handling the case, so I told them about being wanted in another state."

Randy's past had haunted him for a long time. Would those mistakes affect him now? He had served one brief jail sentence for a non-violent crime and been paroled in Arkansas while awaiting trial for forgery of documents. A parole from which he'd walked away.

"That was why you didn't want to go to the police with Willis's identity after you saw him torch the building I was using."

"Well, the detective checked his computer, and I guess Arkansas decided they didn't really want me, because there are no active wants or warrants for me. I don't have to keep a low profile anymore." His smile widened even further. "I'm clear."

Bannister was glad Randy could relax, but he asked a follow-up question that had to be answered. "So, are you ready to turn over a new leaf? Or will you go back to scamming people?"

Randy shook his head no before his boss could finish. "From here on out, I intend to go straight." He paused before continuing. "I have to say that I was glad when you changed the format of the services to a more...a more legitimate one."

"Me, too," Bannister said. "But you have to know that I'm through being 'Brother Bob,' which means you and I both are out of a job. Do you have any idea what you'll do?"

"Actually, I do. One of the detectives I talked to yesterday and again this morning knows a company that's hiring drivers for in-city deliveries."

"But your license—"

"Are you about to ask if I can after being in jail? The detective said I can. I'm not a convicted felon or a warrant-dodger. My record is clean now, and all I have to do is apply and take the tests. I'd have to do that anyway to get a commercial license, so I started the process this morning."

Bannister clapped Randy on the shoulder. "So, you're staying in Goldman?"

"And doing honest work," he responded. "I ... I think I want to hear Dr. Anderson at the First Congregational Church next Sunday." He looked at his former boss. "I believe what he preaches is what I need."

Scott Anderson had been acting as pastor for almost a month, but he still hadn't moved into Ed Farmer's office. Somehow, it didn't seem right. He knew that if he approached Harlan Jones, the chairman of the elders would probably allow him to make the change, but Scott thought it best to leave the office vacant for now. And, of course, when a new pastor came to the church, there'd be the necessity for a switch—if he remained as an associate pastor.

Thus, that Wednesday morning he was working in the glorified office cubbyhole at the church when he looked up to see Abby Davis standing in the doorway.

"May I come in?"

"Of course." He stood and motioned her to a chair across from his tiny desk. When they were both seated, he said, "I've kept up with you through your friends. I hear the surgery went well. And your recovery?"

Abby related the findings in a flat voice, but Scott could see the emotion behind it. "Small tumors on both ovaries, question of spread to tubes. Frozen section showed grade

2 cancer. She did a total removal of ovaries, tubes, and uterus."

"And you're about to start chemo?"

Abby nodded. "I can go back to practice soon. Don't know if or when I'll be able to go full-bore, but I'll do all I can for as long as I can." She paused, then said in a firm voice, "I intend to fight this thing. Mark my words. I intend to make it to the 'five-year survivor' end of the curve."

"We'll be there for you," Scott said.

Abby looked at the books and notes on Scott's desk. "I see you're hard at work on your remarks for the prayer service tonight. Have you decided whether you're leaving the ministry and going back into medicine?"

"Not yet," Scott said. "I'm sort of torn."

"At least you have options," came a voice familiar to both of them.

Scott and Abby turned to see Bob Bannister standing in the doorway.

"I'm sorry," he said. "Your door was open, and I couldn't help hearing the last bit of your conversation." Responding to Scott's gesture, Bannister entered and took the seat next to Abby. He turned toward her. "I'm sorry for your situation. I don't know the details, but I heard enough." Then Bannister looked across to Scott. "And forgive me for my remark about options. It's just that I seem to have run out of them right now."

Scott looked at the two persons seated across from him. "I guess none of us expected to be sitting here under these circumstances right now."

"True," Abby said. "But if I hadn't decided to put an end to my Aunt Kay's nagging, if my primary care doctor at the medical center hadn't done a CA 125 assay, if... Well, if I had waited to seek help the cancer would have had more time to spread before I sought treatment, and I'd be looking at a terrible prognosis. As it is, I've got a fifty-fifty chance to beat this thing. And that's what I intend to do."

Scott turned to Bannister. "Have you come up with anything?"

He shook his head. "No. Randy got some good news though. There are no wants or warrants out for him, and one of the detectives talked to him about a position here as a driver. He's applied for his commercial license already."

"But nothing for you?" Abby said.

"You know, when I talked with Ed Farmer about the 'healing' that wasn't really one, he told me that maybe God had something in store for me. I guess I've taken a couple of steps in that direction, and I'm sure He'll open a path for me soon. But right now, I need a job to pay the bills."

"If you're serious, our custodian at the church gave notice the other day," Scott said. "We'll be hiring a new one."

"Custodian?" The doubt in Bannister's voice was obvious.

"It's actually called a 'facilities engineer.' And it's not someone simply to sweep up and empty the trash containers. We need a person who can be in charge of logistics. Keep things running. Handle problems as they come up."

"That's what I've been doing for years," Bannister said. "Who do I see?"

"Let's talk about it tomorrow."

"What about you?" Abby said. "Any decision on your future?"

"No," Scott said. "My crisis of faith came when the church needed me the most. I don't expect to do more than hold things together until the elders and congregation make the final decision on a new pastor, but there's no telling how long that will take."

"Have you kept your medical license up to date?" Abby asked. "Kept up with CME?"

"Yes, I guess I've always figured going back to medicine was a sort of parachute in case I decided that the ministry wasn't for me."

"If you went back into practice as a surgeon, where would you open an office?" Abby asked.

"I really haven't thought about it," Scott replied. "I came here from Fort Worth, but there's nothing there to draw me back. Besides, there are too many memories of Erica there. One of my professors in med school used to say you should pick an area where you want to be, hang out your shingle, work hard, and you can make a living."

"So why not here?" both Abby and Bannister said almost in unison.

Abby continued. "There's one less surgeon in the area since Willis won't be in practice anymore. And you know the people."

"That's very nice, and I'll keep it in mind, but it's possible God really does want me right here, but doing what I'm already doing," Scott said. "I'll have to take it one day at a time and look for the signposts He puts up."

When both Abby and Bannister left his office, Scott looked at the sheets of notes scattered on his desk. He thought about his first sermon from the pulpit of the First Congregational Church. As the title indicated, he was lost—finally faced with moving forward to a new vocation, but unsure if it was the right move or simply a continued reaction to his loss.

Since then, he'd grown in his relationship with God. Matter of fact, so had Abby Davis and Bob Bannister. Each had experienced an awakening or deepening of their faith, though through different circumstances. As it said in Romans, God could use all their experiences, good and bad, for His glory.

The medicine God had given them was a bitter pill. He hadn't wanted to take it—none of them had—but the growth it brought had been worth it so far. Scott took a deep breath before picking up a clean notepad, ready to start his next sermon.

# # #

Made in the USA
Monee, IL
30 March 2020